Can I Speak My Mind?

Can I Speak My Mind?

Edited by

Neville Raper

Published by Wonderdog Press via Amazon Books

First Published 2018

© Neville Raper 2018

E-mail – Neville.raper@gmail.com

Blogger – The Thoughts of Chairman Anyhow

Contents

About the Author

Neville Raper invented You Tube, has swum the channel twice and is a habitual liar.

He lives in Yorkshire, where just like the locals, he says what he likes and likes what he says.

Broadcaster, Author, blogger, Neville is an occasional stand-up, and regular sit down.

His books are available at all good and bad bookstore, Amazon, Kobo, Barnes Noble and Kindle.

Other Publications –

Nonsense – Anthology 2017

Tales of The Unaccepted – 2017

The Thoughts of Chairman Anyhow – 2017

Tales to Unravel - 2018

COMING SOON

Forget Me Not – Xmas 2018

The Further Thoughts of Chairman Anyhow 2019

Woolworths Fine Dining – 2019

Tales of ? - 2019

Introduction

First, let me thank you for buying this book.

Today you have spent your hard-earned money and, as far as I am concerned, that makes you a hero.

This book is an anthology of work by, and for, people suffering with metal health issues.

It came about due to my partner and I working with various support groups. As a writer and a sufferer, myself I am regularly asked to give talks on how writing has helped me in my battle against the darkness of depression.

Mental health affects 1 in 4 people in the UK alone. It could be your mother, father, brother, sister or you. Along with this, suicide is still the largest killer of men under the age of fifty and, it is increasing.

Whatever your politics, there is no doubt that cuts to mental health services have had a massive impact on sufferers and the support they receive.

I have been heartened by the number of volunteer groups that have sprung up to try and patch up the leaking system. These groups work hard and selflessly to provide support where it's needed, in the community.

As mentioned above, it is no secret that I am a sufferer of depression, I have, as the above statistics confirm, also tried to take my life. I suffer and will always suffer. I know there is no cure, but, there are strategies that help me get through the day.

One of the things that I found helped me was writing. I have always written, mainly jokes and monologues that I used in standup routines or various radio shows I have hosted. But, I'd never written about me.

I started, typically as a man, with a basic list of how I felt on a certain day. I then went back to this on subsequent days to see if I had improved, or not…

After a while, I began adding to my notes. Before I knew it, they started to resemble poetry. I am now three books down with two on the way.

People regularly ask me how writing can help, I will tell you, dear reader, what I tell them.

Within my writing, I have stood on sands on foreign planets, I have fought demons and won, I have seen the glory of love, and I have laughed out loud and shed a tear for characters loved and lost. All this from the comfort of my own laptop.

Pick up a pen…You never know where it may take you. Be good to yourselves, and each other.

Neville

Acknowledgments

I would like to thank all the contributors of this book for submitting their work free of charge for this worthwhile project.

I must personally thank my long suffering better half Von for coming up with the concept for this book, collating the work, dealing with the emails and keeping me in line. Love you. And finally thank you again for buying this collection.

All profits from the sale of this title are being distributed to mental health charities.

All work within this book is the sole property of the individual contributors. All rights are theirs.

If you suffer from mental health issues below is a list of emergency contacts, you can use.

nidirect.gov.uk

Samaritans. Samaritans are open 24 hours a day, 365 days a year, to listen to anything that is upsetting you, including intrusive thoughts and difficult thoughts of suicide and self-harm. Their national freephone number is 116 123, or you can email jo@samaritans.org. Samaritans also offer a Welsh Language Line on 0300 123 3011 (from 7pm–11pm only, seven days a week).

SANEline. SANEline offers emotional support and information from 6pm–11pm, 365 days a year. Their national number is 0300 304 7000.

The Silver Line. If you're an older person (over the age of 55), the Silver Line is there 24 hours a day, 365 days a year to provide information, support and friendship. You can call them from anywhere in the UK on 0800 4 70 80 90 (freephone).

CALM. If you're a man experiencing distressing thoughts and feelings, the Campaign Against Living Miserably (CALM) is there to support you. They're open from 5pm–midnight, 365 days a year. Their national number is 0800 58 58 58, and they also have a webchat service if you're not comfortable talking on the phone.

Nightline. If you are a student, you can look at the Nightline website to see if your university or college offers a night-time listening service. Nightline phone operators are all students too.

Switchboard, the LGBT+ helpline. If you identify as gay, lesbian, bisexual or transgender, Switchboard is available from 10am–11pm, 365 days a year, to listen to any problems you're having. Phone operators all identify as LGBT+. Their national number is 0300 330 0630, or you can email chris@switchboard.lgbt.

C.A.L.L. If you live in Wales, you can contact the Community Advice and Listening Line (C.A.L.L). for a confidential listening and support service. Their number is 0800 123 737 or you can text 'help' to 81066.

I thought I should kick this off with a story of mine. This was first published in my latest book of short stories, Tales to Unravel 2018. It's on Amazon now.

This is a little love story about the power of chips and vinegar…enjoy.

LOVE AND CHIPS

I sit alone and find myself flipping through an old photo album. Kids nowadays don't have such things, photos taken on phones stored to clouds. I wonder if it'll ever rain memories.

I look at the first picture, a slightly yellowed one of me, and my first, and last, love.

Rosemary, my little Rosemary.

For most, I suppose, that name isn't as glamorous as many, but for me it's always been magical.

We met in 1956. I was on holiday with two chums, to a caravan site in the Las Vegas of the East Coast, Cleethorpes. They were great pals, Stanley Bradshaw and Dicky Fletcher. Both dead now of course. Stanley from cancer. Ironically, he never smoked, but his wife, Shirley, had a sixty a day habit. Second hand smoke, first class cancer. Dicky had a dicky ticker, it gave out at fifty-two.

We were on the beach that day. When we'd booked our caravan, we had ideas of nights of debauchery drink and wild, wild women. So far, we'd been here five days and the only thing we'd pulled were cockles from shells.

So, we paraded up and down the East coast beach in our knitted speedos. All three of us knew if we ever got in the sea wearing these things we'd soak up more water than Moses could ever part.

Then I saw her, Rosemary, sitting on the sand with two other friends. Desperately trying to get a tan under an oppressive cloudy canopy. A vision of loveliness a precious stone nestled within the pebbles. I must have walked past her a dozen times sucking in my stomach before she noticed me. She smiled, and the sun came out.

We immediately asked to join them and, to our surprise they said yes. I sat next to Rose, to my relief, she sparked off the conversation.

"The sea's out"

"Yes" I mumbled.

"I wonder how far it goes out?"

"Moscow..." Rosemary burst into musical laughter and that was the blueprint for our love.

I found out, to my joy, that she only lived half an hour from me. So, we started courting.

I used to take the number forty-eight bus to see her. We'd then get the number seven the wheels on our buses went round the town.

Friday, we went dancing. The Mecca Ballroom. The live band trying their best to recreate the sounds coming across the Atlantic, "Long Tall Sally", "Blue Suede Shoes" all sung in broad Yorkshire accents.

How I'd long for the slow dance at the end, a chance to hold my Rose close. To smell her perfume, the warmth of her against me. Where she belonged. We swayed and sighed to "Love me T' ender" The band did try.

On a Saturday night it was the flix. We could never get on the back row, it was always full of writhing snoggers. Every so often the manager would shine his torch on the orgy. The beam like the righteous puritanical stare of a nun, made sure that the ones on the back stopped, and, ironically got none.

We found a quieter spot on the right-hand side. The no smoking section, although cuddled up to my love, I was steaming. We'd watch the films as they came out, The King and I, The Searchers. I enjoyed The Forbidden Planet, and how Rosemary clung to me during the scary parts. During those clinches I usually managed to get sneaky peeks of her bra through the gaps in her blouse. Heaven.

We'd share a bag of chips on the bus back to Rosemary's home. Me, drawing our names in the condensation of the bus's window whilst Rose blew on our super-hot vinegary supper. Our love pronounced backwards to the world.

I'd walk her home and we'd kiss goodnight on her step. If we lingered too long there would be a knock on the window from inside the house. That was my cue to leave. I hardly ever made the last bus and had to walk home. Whatever the weather I was always walking on sunshine.

I'd managed to get a job as a trainee in a local accountancy firm. Cratchet and Scrooge, not quite, but it felt like it. One plus was that they gave me a suit allowance, as long as it was a small check...

Rosemary and I had been seeing each other for about nine months when she suggested I meet her parents. Oh, the terror.

The next Sunday I was invited for Sunday dinner. I was hoping that given Rosemary's stature her parents would be as small as she was, five foot in stocking feet. They weren't, her Dad was a giant. I'm average height, although as I've got older, I've shrunk a bit. I like to say I've downsized. But her father towered above me.

He parents met me at the door, gatekeepers to their daughter. I suppose this was to be my first trial. I'd brought flowers for her mum. As I handed them over with my best set smile I could see where Rose had got her looks. When she smiled she produced the same sun as her daughter did. Her Dad, on the other hand was a different story. I held my hand out in the conciliatory gesture of "I come in peace." The man's hand swallowed mine. His all calloused and worn with manual work, mine soft and pallid in comparison. He gently crushed it.

Rosemary's Mother went to prepare dinner. I sat on the sofa next to my love. I made sure that there was an exclusion zone of at least two feet. Her Dad sat opposite in HIS chair. When do men qualify for their own chair? Do you get it with time? Like a gold watch after so many years devotion.

I never did get my own chair. I preferred to sit with Rosemary. Although I sit alone now.

Her Dad didn't take his eyes off me. Rosemary's Mother's call for her to help her dishing up sent a bolt of frozen fear to my beating heart. I fantasied that whilst they were in the kitchen her Dad would eat ME.

He interrogated me, questions fired, I stammered my responses. Einstein said that time is relative, well, with this potential one it was a lifetime.

I seemed to pass my test, and shortly afterwards Rosemary got to meet my Mum and Dad.

It's funny how in-laws become outlaws and how they mirror each other. Rosemary's Mum loved me, I think the flowers helped, whilst her Dad, obviously did not. I wasn't good enough for his "little princess."

My Dad loved Rosemary, think he fell for that smile as well, whilst My

Mum didn't, Rosemary wasn't good enough for her "little prince."

We married in 1958. A tiny church overfilled with love.

We honeymooned in...are you expecting me to say "Cleethorpes?" Ha, sorry to disappoint you. We upgraded to Bridlington. The one thing I've always heard people say about the place is that "it's flat." Well, it is, in so many ways. Not that we minded. I don't think we saw daylight for five days.

We got a little house, two up one down. I was always afraid that if I slammed the door, it would fall over.

Rosemary went into teaching, I was promoted within the accountancy firm.

We patiently awaited the arrival of the stork. It never arrived.

These were the days before IVF, before egg donors or surrogate mothers. We were sad, of course, but we did what people did then. We shrugged our shoulders, came together as Man and Wife and carried on.

We would have made wonderful parents.

People often asked why we didn't have children, we made our excuses. We never went for tests to see which one of us was to "blame." It wasn't important that we couldn't have babies and that was OUR affair. Eventually people stopped asking.

So, we lived and loved, the time we could have devoted to children we gave to each other. We became involved in local charities, particularly ones for children. Rosemary finally receiving an award at Buckingham

Palace for her service. I was so proud. And through all this time she never lost her beauty. She was my Rose, and by any other name, she would still smell so sweet.

So now I sit, alone, thumbing through frozen snaps of time, reminiscing about all the life and love we shared.

I hear the front door open and close.

"I'm home!"

"Did you get some chips?"

I heard Rosemary laugh, "Yes"

"With vinegar?"

"But of course!"

I still love hot chips.

END

This is Alexandra Carr-Malcolm. In her own words, My name is Alexandra Carr-Malcolm. I was born and raised in Chesterfield, Derbyshire. I now live in Sheffield, South Yorkshire. I work as a freelance British Sign Language Interpreter. I have been writing since my childhood. Five years ago, encouraged by my friends, I set up a poetry blog at www.worldlywinds.com. Most of my poetry is about the human predicament and can be emotive, and at times dark.

Here is a poem by Alexandra titled 'Aduantas'

(Aduantas is an Irish word that doesn't really have an English equivalent but describes that feeling of unease or anxiety caused by being somewhere new, or by being surrounded by people you don't know. It's derived from aduaine, the Irish word for "strangeness" or "unfamiliarity.")

Aduantas

I do not like this place.

I don't belong here,

the stench of death pervades,

yet outside the sun beats down,

hotter than the promised hell.

I do not like this place.

Relics of a bygone day,

guilt and blame pave the way,

to salvation,

but only if you are too weak.

Enough! To believe as

fear holds tight,

demanding allegiance,

to blame and sin;

dragged screaming from within,

without compassion,

or mercy,

for the weak -

end.

I do not like this place,

I do not belong here,

for the stench of death,

offends my soul.

Alice O'Donnell is a graduate of Leeds Beckett University, with a BA (Hons) in English Literature. She is now studying for her MA degree at Sheffield Hallam. Alice is an American born in Maine and had a very famous writer neighbour. She has published several books and they can be found on Amazon.

No Job for Gillian

The phone rang, and Gillian answered it, "What are you wearing Gillian?" The voice said with a heavy Yorkshire accent.

"None of your business," She slammed the phone down. Gillian was shaking as she ran into the living room and checked on her children.

They were fine, sitting, watching tv. Gillian was covered in mess from the day of caring for children and her brown hair was in a sloppy bun. She wiped at her shirt to get the stains off. It was no use, they were embedded. She began to cry.

How had this happened. She thought back on the past few days. Before the phone calls started;

It was just the day before that Gillian had sat mutely and watched her angels sleep. Their arms up at their heads with hands curled inward. Every so often they would suckle as they slept.

She wandered around the house stealthily so as not to wake them up. But, then as she saw them stir. she realised her relax time is over. Katie started to crawl towards her then Michael came behind, then they curled up on her.

Slowly waking up. Their hair was knotted and play clothes unkept.

The CBBE's channel was on in the background, now with no volume as she had turned it off while the kids slept. It was so mind numbing to watch these kids shows. In fact, it was mind-numbing being a child career. She loved her children but yearned for more.

When James came home at night, she could feel him pull away from her mundane conversations. Never anything interesting really. Unlike the person she was before having kids. She had been a hardworking secretary, always on top of the latest conversation buzzing around. She began to cry thinking of her life today. James always smelled so nice and dressed smoothly in a sharp suit.

Gillian surfed through the computer until she came across an advertisement about reading emails to make money. James, her husband, said that she could not make any money while she was home caring for the children. In fact, she was sure that he didn't think she could make any money even without the kids. These thoughts encouraged Gillian to go forth.

She clicked onto the site and then hesitated. Something was nagging at her.   But, she just wanted to check it out, and probably not even continue with it. Gillian searched the site, it just asked for her email address to send her the application. She sent them her details and waited.   Eventually it was sent, and she opened it immediately to have a look.

It seemed straight forward. They asked all kinds of questions. How long she had lived in her previous address? Her phone number, she had guessed that they wanted to know if she would be around for the job.

Then they asked details such as a home address, marriage status and more. She assumed that they just wanted to know how to get in touch with her. Then of course to pay her they needed bank details. This was straight forward. She didn't mind getting money. She filled out the, application.

She took the kids for a long walk before James got home and when she returned she couldn't remember if she had locked the door or not. It was in fact unlocked. She shrugged it off and decided not to tell James about it. He would get so upset.

Gillian's husband, a bank manager, is a hard worker and determined man. He

doesn't trust anyone really. She sometimes wondered if he trusted her. Oh well. She thought about the application form that she was filling out. She would soon show him what she was made of.

As soon as he made it home, he kissed the kids and herself hello then sat down in his office to do his work. He toiled away till dinner time then, after dinner, return to his office. As she sat at her computer a ping came on line. It was a reminder to finish the application form. She quickly finished it and then waited.

Then she realized how late it was getting and decided to go to bed. As she walked upstairs at 9 pm, she stopped by James's office and kissed him good night. She thought that she would have to start her new job tomorrow. James would be proud of her when the first payment arrived.

The next day she went for another long walk and met a friend, Sarah, out in town. Gillian is always so jealous of Sarah, she had no children and always was dressed nicely with her hair brushed smoothly around her shoulders.

They returned to the house and Gillian made them a tea and lunch. Her friend mentioned that she couldn't help noticing that the door was left opened when they were out on the walk. Gillian flushed then said, "I sometimes forget to lock it. Nothing to worry about. I don't think."

James came home, and Gillian tried to talk to him. She realized how boring she sounded and stopped talking, "It's been a difficult day," said Gillian, "Michael's been crying, and I don't know why."

"Sorry," said James, "I'm tired and I've more work to do so…" he moved towards his upstairs office.

"James, I'm trying to talk to you."

"I understand Gillian, but I'm exhausted."

"Maybe we could go upstairs together and discuss this?" she said

James stood silently in front of Gillian. He looked around the corner to see the kids watching tv, "Maybe we could," he smiled at her, taking her hand.

"Come on then let's." Gillian was just about to move closer to James when Katie came around the corner.

They went to bed, but not the way they wanted to, Gillian slept in the guest room so as not to wake James when Michael needed his night time feed. Things were going bad to worse for the two of them.

The house was silent when the phone rang. Gillian looked at the clock, it was 3:00 in the morning.

"Hello."

There was heavy breathing. She hung up, she was numb. She didn't know what to do. Gillian got out of bed to get a drink of water. The phone rang again. She quickly answered it, so as not to disturb James.

"Hello."

"What are you wearing? I'm watching you."

She hung up quickly.

Gillian left the phone off the hook and raced to bed to be close to James. Safe and secure.

She woke early and prepared breakfast for James and the children. She watched the phone while cooking. Then prepared for the moment the phone rang. James was not yet down stairs and she took that opportunity to answer it.

"Hello."

"What are you wearing Gillian?"

"What?" She thought, how does he … how does he know my name?

"Who is this? What do you want from me?"

"I want you …"

She hung up the phone. Quickly and kept it off the hook.

James went to work, and Gillian was left caring for the children.

That day she called Sarah and re explained the past few days to her. How excited she was about the new job and later how that awful man ruined it for her by calling on the phone like that.

"Gillian, you don't think the two are related? You gave them all of your information."

"No."

"Yes," she replied.

"What am I going to do, they still have not called me for my job."

"Gillian, they're not going to call you for your job, there is no job."

James and Gillian's daily routine was repeated as James came home from work. He checked their accounts and noticed that a necklace was bought in Indiana, America. What is this? He showed her and said it was urgent that he contact the bank in the morning.

The following day. While she was alone in the house with the kids, the phone rang.

"Who is this?"

"Your boss. Look outside the door Gillian."

She hung up the phone and then went to the door, carefully, checking through the spy hole. Outside of the door was a teddy bear with a necklace around his neck. She slammed the door and locked it. She ran around the house locking it up. Then ran into the room with her children. She was shaking.

She called her friend Sarah who came right over to bring the teddy bear inside, "You need to call the police, now Gillian."

"What am I going to tell James."

"It is best to come clean with it. Gillian, you must tell him."

"Mummy, can I play with the teddy bear?"

"No, no… darling please go and play," Gillian removed the bear from her grasp and hid it under the counter.

The phone rang again while Gillian's friend was there. Gillian picked up the phone and then as the man was talking into the phone, she screamed. She then screamed, what do you want. Don't you dare call here again."

"But I just wanted to know if you liked the gift?"

"Gillian just hang up," she said.

"No, I want him to stop," Gillian screamed down the phone "Just stop. Do you hear me," She hung up the phone and spent the next hour talking things over with her Sarah?

"Call the number to tell you who called. It's a long shot, but you might get lucky."

Gillian called the number and received the unknown phone number. She called but it went to voice mail, "Ha, so I can reach you too. Don't call me again or I will call the police and give them this number. You will be screwed. DON'T CALL HERE AGAIN."

Night time came but she still hadn't called the police. James came home and informed her that he needed to order them new cards for their accounts as a second item had been bought, a pair of earrings, that very day.

In the morning there was a present on the dresser drawers, she ran to James while opening it. He was still in bed. She kissed him madly,

"What did I do to deserve this?"

She opened the box and saw that it was earrings. She wasn't sure what was going on, "James you shouldn't have."

"I didn't buy those for you," He snorted. James jumped out of bed and raced to his brief case. He read the description of the earrings that had been bought on his credit card.

"Where did you get these from?"

"On the dresser."

She realised then what had happened. She screamed and dropped the earrings on the floor. Gillian ran to James and explained the past week to him. He was furious. He called the police and explained the week to them.

He was so superior to Gillian when he stood in front of her, "There has been someone in our house, while we were sleeping. You have endangered all of us in this house. What did you do, give them the code to our house alarm, hand over the keys to the house to them?"

She begged for his forgiveness, he refused to forgive her. He told her he

couldn't believe he had married such a fool and he wanted a divorce. She stood back, shaking. After dressing he said, "I'll leave you to take care of this business with the police.

As he walked out the door he pulled out his phone, the phone that he had called Gillian on over the past week, at night, and when she was home alone during the day with his children. Ever since he went on her Facebook and email account and saw she filled out that stupid application.

On his way to work he went up to a trash bin and tossed the Pay as you Go phone in it. It had served its purpose. That will teach her to be so sneaky, he thought to himself with a twisted smile on his face.

END

This is Jaki Spencer in her own words - I am age seventy one a full time carer for my husband, my first poem I wrote age nine...but over many sporadic years have penned them. I am a mother of two children, grandmother to four and great grandmother to one. Passionate about the written and spoken word.

This is a great piece espousing the capacity in hope for us all.

RISE UP

You are unique in this world

Don't allow others to put you down.

Stand up be proud of who you represent.

Steadfast in your uniqueness.

If you feel life is sometimes not worth living

Think of what and who means the most to you.

What and whom you would not want to be without.

Let this sustain you, draw on the memories

That did not leave you feeling low and blue.

Let not what is beneath you and behind you,

hold you back like prison bars.

Rise up embrace all you are.

Let this feeling help you to achieve.

Rise up, reach for those glorious stars.

Allow no-one to tell you how to live.

Never hand over the pen for a book on your life

You are the only one that has the words to give

You, are the ink for your pen.

Life is never easy….

There will always be times of struggle.

Frustration and unexpected responsibilities.

Do not isolate yourself in times of trouble.

You have been given a mind – to colour your life.

Choose your options, don't waste your gift.

On what if, or linger on regrets.

You are beautifully unique,

You have within you the ability to take charge,

You will be happiest, by just being you.

Rise up….and believe in yourself.

Be who you are…unique.

Anne Rhodes

This is Anne in her own words. My name is Anne Rhodes. I started writing poetry and stories as a way of clearing my head from fear and pain, a way of filling empty spaces. A way of XXXrealizing that others, as well as myself, suffer (often in terrified silence), a way of telling the world that there is always someone worse off than the reader may ever be. Now I do it simply because I enjoy it!

Nursing, chiropody and historical re-enactment have filled my days, and words have filled my pen. (or rather – have filled my computer!) I think better with a keyboard at my fingers than I do with scrawly writing done by hand.

I'm a mother, a grandmother, not as fit as I was (physically), not quite lost it (mentally) – at least I hope not!

Despair

I cannot even describe to myself
How I feel
So, therefore, how can I explain to you?
Dejection
Bites into my heart, my soul, my being.
Misery
Envelops me within its heavy folds.
Wretchedness
Is merely the despondency of mind
Painfully
Etched deep into the very breath I breathe.
Gloom-laden
Darkness blocks out all hope of empathy.
Disturbance
Of the mind they say – no, of the very
Tormented
inner-core of life itself afflicted
And mourning.
Desolation comes in waves so deeply
Foreboding
I despair of being able to speak
Openly
Of this despair which grips my mind and heart.

This is a heart-breaking true story about a mother and her battle with postnatal depression.

The writer has asked to remain anonymous.

Beyond the Baby Blues

I am a 39-year-old stay-at-home mum from Barnsley. In my spare time I like to read, write and draw. I was around 6 months pregnant with my second child when I started to feel odd. Really weepy and down on everything. I just put it down to pregnancy hormones (as did everyone else) I gave birth to my daughter by C-section. Pre-planned as she was breech.

From the moment I saw her I felt absolutely nothing. No rush of love. No affection. Horrible, right? That's what I thought. That first night I said she could go to the nursery because I thought I was just tired. That night I cried for my mum.

The next morning, when the nurses brought my daughter to me I was so angry, but I never said anything. I just acted like everything was normal. Just a happy mum, welcoming her baby. But inside I was so depressed. I went home three days later, and I really struggled. I'm ashamed to say, I turned to alcohol to try and help me feel better. Still not saying anything to anyone about how I felt.

I used to cry to my baby, saying I didn't want her. I didn't know what to do. After a few weeks the paranoia set in. I thought, because she had gone to the nursery that first night that the hospital had given me the wrong baby. I was absolutely convinced! But still I carried on and didn't say a word.

After a few months, my family noticed I wasn't getting better and I was drinking more than I should. I finally broke down and owned up to what I was going through. But I didn't tell them everything.

They all thought it was a throwback to when I had my first child at eighteen, who is Down's (but that's another story). When I heard that I felt so sorry for him that I resented my baby even more. I was forever apologising to him even though he was only five years old. I just wanted to take him and get away from it all.

The drinking continued. I got more paranoid. I stopped eating because I thought everyone was trying to poison me because I didn't want my baby.

At the time I thought it was all true.

I don't remember exactly when I started to think normally but I think my daughter was around two-year-old.

A long time to have postnatal depression, right? Yeah, a lifetime. But I came out the other side

This is Jason Ginnelly. In his own words -

I'm 43 and I've personal experience of mental health matters from my own clinical depression which, I've had to deal with most of my life.

I've been affected by several painful life events that have damaged and battered the armor I wear out in the world to shield and protect me as best it can but sometimes, the hurt and pain seeps through and has left indelible marks emotionally.

A few years ago, I worked in the private sector in mental health counselling as a support worker. I covered various roles and tasks as a counsellor. One thing I always felt moved by was, the reflection back from people who shared their pain with me. The people I helped appreciated the empathy they received from me, as I'd been through what they had, and was not just quoting help from a book.

I enjoy writing and find I no longer feel I need to dismiss or hide away my talent.

I write short stories, scripts, poetry and do longer form writing including on a script for a play / drama in memory of my late father.

Here is a poem from Jason about the constant battle within the mind.

Mind.

Thinking and feeling, its pulsing and spinning,
My mind inside, it's never fully known healing.

A head full of words, actions, reactions, dithering and inaction.
Crying out against the white noise inside and out,
Coping on the surface on a scale of 1-10...
Gulping hard for air, hyperventilating.
Guttural growling growing...unrelenting.
Emotional belongings packed up tightly against the storm force feelings that
ensue.

Memories happiness, coping fractured,
Fragmented recollections, sadness, heartache,
BANG, chasm splits...

Mind is slipping, sliding, slithering, and writhing on the shattered shards of
internal glass.
Searing pain the feeling now,
From the slashing and slicing of the knife, knife, knife.

Invisible, visible scars, lost in space, languishing in a void, mirror reflections
etched on my face.
Unseen to the outside world, catastrophe and wreckage inside of untold mind
violence.

Are you living or existing?
After retreating inside to try and heal the self,
My eyes are being punished now, blinking hard at the daylight.
Thrashing through trash of what's left of disintegrated me,
Covered in cobwebs, debris and dust.

Gathering together dishevelled remnants of my elegant clutter.
Reset to default position,
Harmonic waves and old songs playing,
Internal radio forever needs retuning.

Uncomplicated normality, the need for clarity, healing and thought.
Coping on the surface on a scale of 1-10...
Tremor in the talking,
Eye contact, please non binding.

A mind inside, thinking and feeling,
Will it ever fully know healing?

Barry Fentiman Hall

Barry Fentiman Hall (BFH) is a writer based in the Medway region of Kent. He is primarily a poet of place. He has been published in several journals such as Anti-Heroin Chic, I Am Not A Silent Poet, and Crack The Spine. His debut solo collection The Unbearable Sheerness Of Being was published by Wordsmithery in 2015. His latest book England, My Dandelion Heart has just been launched (Wordsmithery 2018). He is also the host of Roundabout Nights, Chatham's oldest regular live lit night and the editor of Confluence Magazine. He has a thing for hares.

This is a beautiful metaphorical piece to our canine keeper.

GREY DOG

3am is lightless
Reflection is all
It can shed on
The dream walks
Of the sleeper
Clad in shallow sand
Feeling in the bone
How cold it can get
This far from the sun

Hearing the sigh
Of black dog breath
Warm at the heel
I turn and face him
This sad familiar
Damp before dawn
And downlit limp
Shivering grey with
Remembered regret

That is the colour
Of history haunting
The heart that flies
With the horseshoes
Fitful at things that
Are done with now
But he is faithful
This sad eyed boy
He stays in step

He is not midnight
And cannot bite
This washed out
Shadow cast thin
On ungiving ground

Half life lived fast
Burned at my heels
He won't catch me
I am too fast for him

Reckoning sunwise
I fly from green hills
With the starlings
Laughing at buildings
Gone Neanderthal
Tripping on earth gas
Black dog grey gone
He will be back
But he has lost this one

This is Elisabeth Straw, in her own words…I am a writer, a teacher and an examiner. I write everything from non-fiction articles on educational issues, autism and gardening to social media strategies and fictional writing. I recently completed my first novel; Control. Alt. Delete. It's an inspirational story of a woman who becomes a victim of coercion and control and how she manages to escape and survive. I'm married, and I live with my husband, two children and two cats, Barbara and Mittens in South Yorkshire. I'm a champion of autism and I advise parents who are going through the EHC system. I've been a teacher in a wide range of roles in a variety of educational settings for over twenty-five years. I love teaching and if I can pass on my love of literature and writing then I am happy!

Elisabeth has a successful blog where she showcases her work and other fascinating subjects. You can find it on the following link :- writeonejaleigh.wordpress.com

This is a lovely written little tale about… well, life will always find a way.

Be Careful What You Don't Wish For

He was meant to be arriving on Friday at seven pm, by nine there was no sign of him. I'd gone to a lot of trouble, making lamb shanks. As the lamb juices dried up and dinner began to ruin, then so too did any thought of a decent weekend.

He wasn't really my type but surely it was better to have someone than no one? I preferred someone a bit more refined. He'd built up a plumbing empire throughout the Wirral, '*U-Bend – I Fix.*' Lots of double entendres about unblocking pipes but oh how rough were his hands!

We'd had the craziest of first dates in which I drank far too much prosecco and ended up going back to his hotel room. Then the oysters we'd eaten caused him to throw up, I made my excuses and left. We'd seen each other a few times since. We never did discuss if we were an item.

He called to apologise about ten. By this time. I had had most of a bottle of champagne and was feeling sorry for myself. I don't know why I said it. I really wasn't that into him. I am not sure if it was just me being an attention seeker, but I told him I was pregnant.

'I thought you were on the pill. '

'I must have slipped up.' I confided. I left him to mull it over as I drank the last of the bottle and collapsed on my bed.

I awoke to find fifty missed calls and a bunch of messages. I could hear someone banging loudly. I was shocked to see him at the door with a paper bag.

'I had to come when you said you were …… I need to know. This could change the rest of my life.'

I was regretting it more and more now.

'We tried for years and had IVF. None of it worked. I was told I would never have children. I need to know. For certain.' He offered me the paper bag.

I had got myself in a spectacular mess. He would go mad when he realised I was telling porkies. I was racking my brains. Did I know anyone who was pregnant who could come to the house and take the test for me? Should I just call my Dad over in case he became aggressive when he discovered I had tricked him? I tried dithering, 'I've already had my morning wee. It might not show up just yet.'

He pushed me into the bathroom and shut the door.

I took the cap off the test and attempted to hold it over the toilet bowl. Two minutes it would take. I looked around wondering if it might be an idea to try and escape out of the bathroom window. The first blue line appeared telling me the test had been successful. I opened the door and pushed the test towards him as I bowed my head. He started shouting but with joy? I snatched the test back and looked at it, baffled. And then there it was: the second blue line.

–

This is Frank Varley... in his own words. I'm 59 yr. old, semi-retired from Leeds who ends up doodling with words. I can't really consider myself a writer and apart from my deep love of sprouts, there's not much to tell.

This is a great humorous poem about the festive season.

A Christmas Poem

Sprouts they are delicious

Sprouts they are supreme

Boiled and boiled and boiled

To me they are a dream

Sprouts I have them every year

Come rain or come shine

A green globe of deliciousness

Upon which to dine

It wouldn't be the same without them

That Christmas dinner plate

Those sprouts are there because

They make me salivate

So, when I'm asked how many

My wife should give to me

I say I think I'll be able to manage

A total of three..........

But I left two of them.

Here is Jason again with a great poem comparing mental health to the crash of a computer.

Your mind is Your computer...

...System access set up...

Battery life 100% fully functioning...

Mother Board = Perfect...

Central Processing Unit = Complete...

initialising introductory protocols ...

formatting set up and data transfer...Buffering...

information downloaded...

software ready for programming and operating tasks...

Action, Reaction, cause, effect...Thought...Buffering....

Reflection, introspection...Buffering...Reflection, thought...thought...

Action, reaction, cause effect, reflection...Buffering...

Data analysis suggested...security protocols checked...

Firewall safety and maintenance procedures required...

Buffering...thought, reflection, introspection...reaction, action, cause and effect...Buffering...

cause, effect, thought, reaction, introspection, action, thought, reflection...Buffering...

virus detected...thought, thought thought...Buffering...

operating suggestions questioned...Buffering...

Return to original default settings...Buffering...

Control, Alt, Delete...Control, Alt, Delete...Buffering...

thought, though, thoug, thou, tho...Buffering...

cause, effect, reflection...introspection...Buffering...

hardware system malfunction detection...Mood drop...repair...

access, describe, prescribe...Pill Pop...Buffering...

Defragging...thought, thought, though, thoug...reflection...action, reaction...Buffering...

close all existing open programs running...Buffering...

Reboot required...updates and restart required...Buffering...

Mother-Board no longer operable...

Central Processing Unit...requires operator analysis...Buffering...

Storage systems require memory upgrades...Buffering...

Reflection inspection...thought, introspection, thought, action, reaction, cause and effect...Buffering

Files available to upload...Buffering...Reflection, thought...introspection...thought... thought...Buffering...

unable to download...unable to complete tasks...

Try removal of used / unused data, that may have corrupted the memory...Buffering...

Buffering...Buffering...Buffering...

original system and programming no longer supports existing model and current set up...

contact manufacturer for advice and latest compatible operating versions...

Battery life discharging...Reconnection to energy / power supply and technical support advised and recommended.

thought, action, reaction, reflection, introspection...cause and effect...Buffering...

thought, action, reaction, thought, cause and effect...thought, reflection, introspection...Buffering...

Sharon Shields

Sharon Shields is a prize-winning author from Wakefield. Ok, it was only for the most atmospheric writing at Mirfield Show 2018, but hey, we've all got to start somewhere! She loves her daughter, her dog and Greg Davies, but not necessarily in that order. In fact, probably not in that order. She is just starting a creative writing degree.

This is a great short story unusually told from the point of view of the abuser. Many men hide their talents for abuse behind a winning smile, Sharon's character is one of those.

A Leopard Never Changes its Spots

My key didn't fit. I took it out of the keyhole and looked at it in surprise. I turned it over, held it up to the light, even shook it but it was the right key. Mortice key for the back door, yale for the front. It was the yale. I didn't understand. I took a step back and scratched my head, looked at the key again, looked at the door again. I must have put it in the lock the wrong way, I'd better try again. Didn't want to make too much noise though and wake her up, I couldn't cope with the drama. I put the key in, turned it, nothing. I just didn't get this. Why didn't it fit? Stuff it, it was a warm night, I'd sleep in the back garden; it wouldn't be the first time.

"Oi," I felt a kick in my ribs, hard enough to wake me but not hard enough to do any damage. "Get out of my garden, you pisshead!"

I was awake now. That was a man's voice. Calling my garden his. Not bloody likely. "Get lost, mate, it's my garden. YOU'RE in the wrong garden. Idiot..." I stopped speaking. This wasn't my garden. Well it was: I'd put that shed up in the corner when we'd first moved in, planted that cherry tree and laid that patio. But that table and chairs weren't mine and I'd certainly never had an umbrella. I didn't want to hide from the sun, I sat in it as often as I could. With a beer, usually two.

"I don't know what the hell is going on here. What are you doing? Get out of my way."

I pushed past him; I was going inside to find her, have it out with her, see who this idiot was in my house.

I got as far as the door.

"I don't think so, pal". A hand grabbed my collar and hauled me backwards. I struggled a little, just to try and save face, but I knew I wouldn't get past him.

"Alright, alright, get your hands off, I'm not going in. I just wanna know where she is. Is she in there? Stop hiding, I only want to talk!" I shouted the last bit loud enough for her to hear; she'd be out, she never could resist me, even like this. Our bedroom window creaked open, I knew she'd been waiting for the right moment. A tousled-haired brunette leant out, rubbing her eyes against the brightness of the morning. "Wha'sgoin'on" she mumbled.

"Who the hell are you?" I took a step back to get a clearer view. I turned back to look at the idiot. Something was not right here. I shook my head hard and felt his grip tighten on my collar. Had I banged my head? "Where is she? Where's Lucy?" My eyes swam with tears, my head pounding from last night in the bar. "Where's my Lucy?"

I felt the grip relax. "Lucy? As in Smith?"

I sniffed quietly. "Of bloody course, who did you think I was talking about? Where is she?"

"You don't know? I'm sorry pal, I don't know who you are but by looking at the state of you I'd guess you're that lowlife pisshead she was with. Hit any other women lately?" He took a step towards me, fist raised, eyes bright with a barely controlled temper. I recognised it, it looked back at me from the mirror every morning.

"Fuck off! I slapped her once, well maybe twice. I didn't mean it, she knew that. It was just the beer and her nagging. I didn't mean it." I took a step back; his fist was still raised. "What has it got to do with you anyway? Are you shagging her as well? I knew she'd got some idiot on the go. I wasn't standing for that. No way. But I showed her. Give her a slap, didn't I."

I didn't see his fist move, but I felt my nose explode. I dropped to the floor, curled up like a foetus, like the baby she said she'd lost.

"Get out of my garden and don't you dare come back. No wonder she moved away, you bastard."

I felt the grip on my collar again and curled tighter. I could taste blood and I didn't want to be hit again. I felt him drag me down the path. "Now git!" He threw me out onto the pavement. My head bounced off the tarmac, adding to the ringing in my ears.

"Yeah, well you can keep this shitty house" I shouted to his retreating back. "Never liked it here, anyway!"

"Mr Smith, I'm afraid I'm not at liberty to give you any information. Mrs Smith returned the keys a month ago."

I despised the middle-aged woman behind the counter. She peered at me over the top of her glasses like a spinster primary school teacher. But I had to play the part.

"I've been away, see, and when I got back she was gone. I miss my wife and I just want to see her." I sniffed and dabbed at the corner of my eye, wiping away an imaginary tear.

She continued looking at me, completely unmoved by my performance. "Hmm, I understand you've been 'away'." She emphasised the final word. It was obviously written in the file in front of her. "Well I'm sorry, Mr Smith. Your wife didn't leave a forwarding address. I can be of no further help."

I had to up my performance.

"I know I did something wrong, something terrible. I didn't mean to hurt her. I was upset. Someone had told me she was seeing someone else. That the baby wasn't mine. I didn't mean to hurt her or the baby. She fell down the steps. I tried to catch her, I really did. I just want to see my wife." I put my head in my hands, pretended to sob. Women always fell for this rubbish. I separated my fingers and peered through.

"Goodbye, Mr Smith."

I knocked on my probation officer's door. I didn't like her, patronising bitch, but I had nowhere else to go. No-one else wanted to know me, not after what had happened.

"Come in." Her cheery, saccharin voice grated on my every nerve. "Now, what's the matter, Brian? I didn't expect to see you just yet; our first meeting isn't for a couple of days. What can I do for you?"

"Erm, my wife is missing. Like, our house isn't our house anymore. I need to find her. I need to talk to her. We need to get this sorted so we can get on with our lives. I wanna try for another baby. I love her. I tried the Council, but the Housing Department couldn't tell me anything. Can you help me? I'm begging you." I lowered my head and wiped away another imaginary tear.

"Now, Brian, let's start at the beginning, and this is important. Where did you spend the night? Your parole was approved with you spending the night at your home address. I need to find you a hostel or some other accommodation for tonight. Let's see what I can do."

I ended up getting a room in a parole hostel. I hated it; it was full of men like myself, half of them trying to make amends, half of them working towards their next crime. But all of them were bigger than me. I hated it and had to get out. I had to find Lucy, persuade her I was a reformed man and move back in with her. It would be all too easy once I found her. She loved me, and she'd let me do anything. I just needed to find her. She didn't really have any family nearby, so I just needed to work out where she'd be.

I tried to find her on Facebook first; she'd always been a big user of that, sharing stupid memes about love and other such rubbish. Could never figure it out myself, why would you want everyone to know your business? But it had given her, something to do and I'd left her to it. I'd checked her phone a couple of times to look at it when she'd gone out of the room, but it was just her talking to her mates about their kids, so I'd stopped looking after a while. Maybe I should've checked again, see if she really was seeing someone else like I'd been told.

I logged into an account I'd set up but never really used and searched for her. Nothing. The only people with the same name lived in America and didn't look like her. She would never have come off Facebook. Maybe I could find her through her friends, one of them must know where she is.

I checked three of her closest mates. They all had their pages set so I couldn't see their friends. That was no bloody use, what the hell were they playing at?

Maybe if I rang them I could make them believe I was a reformed character, sorry for all I'd done and ready to make amends. I rang Claire first, her best friend since school. The phone rang and rang but she didn't answer. Cow always had her phone in her hand and now she was ignoring me. I wasn't having that, but I'd check Emma and Dawn first.

Emma's phone went straight to voicemail and Dawn's number didn't exist anymore, I got the same dead tone noise as when I'd tried Lucy's number. I wasn't standing for this; bloody witches had ganged up on me.

I tried Claire's house first, she wouldn't be expecting that. I strode up the garden path and brayed on the front door. I heard her stupid little dog barking somewhere inside the house, heard a stifled "shurrup" and the dog stopped barking. So, we were playing that game then, were we? I hammered on the door again.

"Claire, I know you're in. I want to talk to you. I only want to find Lucy. I love her, I want to be with her. Come on, Claire, you've known her the longest. You know me and her were good together. Come on, love, I only want to talk."

Not a noise came from the house. Not a movement, nothing.

"Come on now, Claire. If you're not coming down, at least tell her I want to talk to her, yeah?"

Emma lived around the corner from Claire, so I guessed I'd try there next.

I knocked on her door, not too aggressively, this time I had to appear contrite.

"Emma," I called through the letterbox when she didn't answer after my second knock. "Look, if you're in, will you tell Lucy I need to see her? I just want to have a little chat, a catch up, yeah? Look, just tell her I miss her, and we can work this out. Tell her she can ring me anytime."

I felt a hand grab me from behind. Shit, not again.

"Look, dickhead, leave Emma alone, it's nothing to do with her. Just go."

I recognised the voice. Emma's bloke was huge, I had no intention of arguing with him, but I had to pretend. I struggled slightly against his grip.

"Look mate, I only want to find Lucy, I'm not here to cause any trouble, I just want to see my wife."

"Well, she ain't here so fuck off, dickhead."

He spun me on my feet and marched me out of the garden.

"Alright, mate, I'm going. Tell Emma I called round, yeah?"

His grip loosened slightly. I turned my head as much as I could.

"Look, mate, I shouldn't be saying this," he hissed "I know where she is. Emma has sworn me to secrecy, but shit, why shouldn't I tell you. She's your wife, right? All I know is she's got a house, shacked up with a bloke, around the corner from her mother. But remember, I didn't tell you."

He let go of my collar and I dropped to my knees. He leant forward, "Remember what I said, I didn't tell you." He straightened up. "Now go!" he yelled, aware that people could be watching.

I scrambled to my feet, half running, desperate to keep up the pretence, but my heart was bouncing in my chest.

I stood at the corner of the mother-in-law's street. I scanned the road quickly, hoping that she wouldn't see me. She was a nasty cow, had hated me on sight, and the feeling was mutual. I bet she'd loved it when Lucy had moved back here. Away from my clutches. Well, she was in for a shock. I didn't believe for a second that Lucy was with someone else, she loved me too much to do that.

I saw the curtains twitch on a house to my right. No doubt some nosey old busybody, but it was a good place to start.

"Hi" I forced my face to smile at the grey-haired woman in front of me. "I wonder if you can help me? I'm looking for an old school friend, Lucy. She came from round here but I'm not sure where she is now. Have you seen her?"

She leant on the door frame, sucking on her toothless gums. "Erm, there's a Lucy Jones on the next street, her mam also lives round here. Don't think she's been back here long though. They say that the bloke she was married to used to knock her about. Been in prison apparently, nasty sod by all accounts.

They say she lost a baby when he pushed her down the stairs. I hope he rots in hell. Prison's too good for people like that. In my day, the lads round here would've sorted him out. He wouldn't have done it again, that's for sure."

I tried my best to look both shocked and saddened, but I had to hurry her up. "Oh my god, how awful, poor Lucy. So, where did you say you say she lived?"

The woman squinted at me, her eyes locked onto mine. "Here, you're not him, are you? I've said too much. I'd better go back inside." She started to back away. I smiled and gently rested the tips of my fingers on her arm.

"No, no I'm not. Lucy was so lovely at school, it's such a shame she ended up with someone like that. I hope she's ok now. It sounds like she's better off without him."

I felt her arm relax under my touch.

"She is; evil so and so that he is. Anyway, you're nothing like him, I can tell. You wanted to know where she lives? Round the corner, number 3. She should be in at this time, she's got a chap now, but I don't think he's there, I saw him walk past earlier. There again, you can't miss him, big lad he is. Runs the gym on the high street."

I tensed, I didn't like the sound of him, but if he wasn't there I'd go round now. She'd see me, I knew she would.

"Thank you, Mrs, err?"

"Gordon. Joan Gordon."

"Well thanks again, Mrs Gordon, I'll pop round now, seeing as I'm here. I'll meet her chap later, no doubt. Bye, you take care now."

"Bye now."

I marched up to number 3 and banged my fist as hard as I could on the door, feeling a flash of excitement as I heard her voice call "Just a minute, I'm coming! I wasn't expecting you home yet."

She pulled the door open quickly, "Did you forget your…" the words dried on her lips as she say me, her mouth dropped open.

"Hi sweetheart, missed me?" I took a step forward, my foot already on the threshold.

"Shit!" she tried to push the door shut, but I put all my weight on my front foot.

"Don't you want to see me? Scared lover boy might come home? Well that's not fucking likely, that old bitch around the corner says he's at work. Aren't you going to invite me in?" I shoved the door on the last word and Lucy fell back against the stairs, landing on her back, the force knocking the breath out of her. I kicked the door shut behind me.

"Ready to go upstairs already? And I haven't even been home five minutes. Come on then, give your old man a kiss first, god I've waited for this for so long."

I looked at her on the stairs, her arms across her chest, silent tears on her cheeks.

I moaned and moved towards her, unbuckling my belt with one hand, enjoying the fear on her face. She wasn't moving away, she still wanted me, I knew she would. This had been far easier than I expected.

I heard a roar behind me, felt the air pressure change as the door banged flat against the hall wall. I felt myself being lifted into the air.

"Get off her, you bastard! Lucy, go upstairs, go into the bedroom and shut the door. This won't take long."

I was unceremoniously thrown out of the door, catching my head on the door frame. I landed hard on the lawn.

"Thought you'd get away with this, did you?" I felt a kick in my ribs, heard the air leave my lungs. "Good job Mrs Gordon realised who you were and rang me at the gym." Kick. "You absolute bastard." Another kick, this time between my legs. I vomited instantly.

"Oh dear, did that hurt? Well now you know how Lucy felt. You know, when you pushed her down the stairs and killed her baby." I curled up into a ball, waiting for the pain to subside, waiting for the next kick.

"Now fuck off and don't come back. If I ever see you again, ever hear your name, even hear that you've thought about Lucy, I'll kill you." He pulled me

to my feet, leant in until his nose nearly touched mine. "Do. You. Understand?"

I gulped and nodded, fighting down the nausea.

He let go of me, giving me another kick as I crawled along the garden. I spat a final acidic mouthful of spit onto the grass and pulled myself to my feet. "Don't worry, I won't be back. You can keep her, frigid bitch."

I scuttled down the road until he was out of sight. I could see a pub ahead of me, I'd go in there, clean myself up a bit, have a beer or two to calm my nerves.

The barmaid was slim and blonde, just how I liked them. I turned on my best, full voltage smile. She blushed and lowered her eyes.

"Hi, gorgeous. I'll have a beer please and whatever you want." I extended my arm across the bar. "My name's Brian. What's yours?" She giggled, held my hand a fraction too long. "Hi, I'm Adele. Lovely to meet you."

I grinned. This was going to be easy.

This writer wishes to remain anonymous but, she does tell us that she is 34 from West London and has been writing for herself on and off since her early teens.

Here is poem of how depression can, and does, make you feel. It is a sad and beautiful piece of writing

Blow me away, please.

Take me with you as you whistle your tune.

Wrap me in your treachery.

Engulf me.

I need the air.

Fresh, sweet, beautiful air

to breathe into my miserable bones.

I feel like I'm decaying, crumbling into nothing.

A pile of old musty clothes kicked to a corner in the loft.

Dusty and suffocating.

Help me escape,

I'll ride on your coattails.

Fly and twist and turn, like a bee released from behind a window pane.

Help me feel light, not weighed down by the beast within.

Don't let me crash, and fall, and sink.

This is 'Master Flzent Ceeple' who is 27 and from South Yorkshire. In his own words;

What got me interested in writing was having a good sense of humour, so in the start of summer 2012 I started to write jokes. I then wanted to test my ability & with a wide taste in music & Christmas 2013 approaching, I got into song writing. I started with part covers, then my own. By February 2015 I'd written 22 songs. So I started with poetry, where the 22nd song became the 1st poem, so poetry was the next step. Following note making on the 5th poem I realised its potential & a series of stories followed shortly after.

In winter 2016, I started some side story tales alongside creating the intro for my 1st story. I was lucky enough to receive some great support, help and advice from Hive South Yorkshire and Verse Matters. This encouraged me to pick up the pen and venture into poetry once again. I managed to complete 20 poems in 21 days. I have now created 29 poems

My writing is important to me, equally as are my drawings & edits, they're my biggest interests alongside fictional & fantasy stories, plus magic & its tricks or treats. I like to draw uniquely for my world, as it helps me see more than what I can & engage more. I have 6 Zeensimor poems, with another 4 pending. It's so much fun

More work by 'Master Ceeple' can be found on his successful blog - mysticaltreeandbeyond.wordpress.com

'Master Ceeple' has created a new world to encompass his writing, he calls it Zeensimor. Here is his unique piece.

The World of Zeensimor

Magic is great, especially with spells such as the lifting charm of Cloudothi Lifosa, created by Sir Vok Fosar, shortly after his accident of falling whilst on the mountain of Svent Turi, south east of Zeensimor Central.

Then there's the funny Snoofi Trepted hex, which makes you sneeze and leak snails and dirt from your nose and ears, such a laugh, but brings a blotch of hissing blue gunk instead of tears and woes when you cry.

The most mischievous is the Ast Hu-Qi jinx, the exact definition is unknown, only its three creators the three troublesome triplets, the Floffuri brothers Luke, Cain and Crutt know, they also created the Allceae curse, which's a constant stream of farts, runny, wheezy and skunk-like of different sound levels. The last is the Zingceae curse, a painful set of hiccups, sometimes with fizzing puke; thankfully a few healing charms were formed such as the Gijian, which helps with sickness that was placed by wickedness.

There was also the Elbcus, which was to help recover from colds for those visiting the ice of Vells Glacier in the North West.

Now amongst the triplet's parts of fun, danger wasn't of concern to them, which is why the Comkown healer was quickly whipped up, as we all need wounds and bones seeing to.

At the side of these spells is the natural magic of adult butterflies gathering on Wongst Rocks to watch their children being hatched from the Counds eggs, and then there's the stormed colour change of scenery through the rainbow drops.

Seeing the underground living/flying Oskiff as it hops around in thin air and not forgetting others of spending time with a Dektol tree, so comforting and a great shade from the sun plus a lovely spot for a picnic. But for me, my favourite is petting the Tups. Though a slight nuisance, these neon multi-coloured fur balls are so gentle and can help with any ripped clothing. They tend to attract Tinics, which are never lonely as they travel in packs and repairany cracks in the paths, bridges and extraordinary vehicles around all Zeensimor, which are commonly used by the ground keepers of Cler Talso.

Quigly Flural, Sox Patoll, Daced Ragic and the king of the crops Gend Fuffers, they keep a close eye on the insects crawls, tracks and where they decide to take their baths, now whether it be high or low, people often stare as work's carried out, but it's a unique place, so all's different, no one's ever slandered, it's all equal here, there's rarely anything to fear and when there is, we're all here in support.

We're friendly and full of inviting smiles, you'll see for yourself as you can cross the bridge of trickery tiles, just don't be scared, as the whiff of fear will be sensed. We know that doesn't seem fair, but we keep away the trouble bound, we're a cultural diversity world, if you don't like it and present this, then enjoy the torture on Mercury.

The Ceeple monsters are very lairy, so much so, you won't win, especially as you'd be very wary and your silly trot won't work, am not trying to scare you off, am just stating that we're equal and strive for happiness, tranquility and adventure like no other, we don't have a boss, we have a creator who lives like us, whether a Teenery, Leerers, Puver, Lecks, Crich, Mewcles or Nure, we're all the same, please come visit us, the password is 'biscuits'.

Watch out for those Mhollous monsters,

Yours Sincerely,

Flzent, the Ceeple Gnomes & Groundskeepers.

This is Marjorie Lacy. In her own words:

We, my husband Roy and I, for most of our adult life, were self-employed, both in wholesale and retail of such diverse products as Cosmetics to Hardware and Ironmongery. I went from teaching manicure to hairdressers to weighing out nails at the shop counter.

I retired 10 years ago at the age of 69 and began reading through a Reading Group, I joined a Creative Writing Course and have been attending that for the last ten years. It was a surprise to me that I could write poetry and prose. Because there was not one, I began a monthly Poetry Group at South Elmsall Library which is still going strong. I encourage everyone I meet to read and write! It will at least, keep everyone out of mischief and make a lot of lovely friends.

Last year, with the help of my husband we self-published a poetry book. Which was very exciting especially when people who bought it enjoyed my work.

I also review new and debut fiction books for Publishers. My slogan is, "Readers are Writers and Writers are Readers

This is a fantastic autobiographical piece dripping with wonderful nostalgia.

My Mum's confused.......

We knew mum had started being a bit strange. She lived in Leeds; we lived 25 miles away near Pontefract. She started phoning us saying 'the T.Vs. gone off' or things like 'the light won't go on.' I had no alternative but to make the fifty-mile round trip to put the T.V. back on or change a light bulb

One day she phoned to say, 'the Post Office won't give me my pension.' Off I went to sort it out. When I got there the assistant explained, 'Your mum's already collected her pension and been in three more times asking for it.' She did add that they thought mum was badly confused. By this time, I had come to the same conclusion.

When I returned mum's Library books for her, the Librarian said, 'I'm glad you've come in, I want to talk to you about your mum. Do you know how confused she is?' She offered me an envelope with notes in it. 'Your mum has only been using £10.00 notes as bookmarks! We've collected them all together.' When I checked the envelope, there was more than £100.00 in it. How kind the Library staff had been in keeping them for mum.

It was apparent that I needed to do something. Mum was medically checked over, I enlisted the help of Social Services, both in Leeds and my local area. Once the diagnosis of Alzheimer's Disease was confirmed, arrangements were put in place for her to live near me in a Pensioner bungalow. Privately, I worried she would not survive the move; she was 83 years old. She did. Her home in Leeds was a through Terrace House, one side was opposite a builders yard. At the other side, the Conservative Club overlooked her living room and kept out a lot of light. Her new home had a tree-lined street and farmer's fields nearby. She took herself on little walks to see them, giving her lots of pleasure.

Mum had attended the Methodist Church all her adult life, I contacted the nearest Methodist Church, where they welcomed her with open arms. They could not believe she was suffering from Dementia. Because she could read aloud from the Bible in a good clear voice, and was able to sing hymns from memory. I realised then, how she was adept at hiding her condition. If anyone spoke to her, she would nod and smile. I learned that with Alzheimer's disease, music is the last memory to go.

Three times a week she was picked up and taken on a tour around the local area picking up other pensioners, arriving at a Day Centre for a meal. Afterwards they did craft activities, making memory boxes and other small items. They were all taken home again, dropping off in reverse order. Mum thought that she had been taken around the Yorkshire Dales, enjoying a good meal at a hotel. She always commented on the lovely scenery. Mum never found out that the Day Centre was only five minutes away from her house; telling me how beautiful the views were.

Other comic events that made us smile, if mum had not liked the sandwich that I or the daily carers made for her, she would hide them in the oven. I only discovered the discarded food when we ran out of plates and I had a hunt around for them.

One morning, I had lifted some bread out of the freezer to thaw out for tea time. When I returned I couldn't find the bread, I asked mum she replied, 'I don't know what you did with the bread, it's all wet. I've hung it out on the line to dry.' When I looked out of the window, there was a row of slices of bread neatly pegged out on the line!

Other issues over the bread, she loved to feed the birds, often I would arrive to find no bread at all as she had fed the full loaf to the birds. I would have to go to the shop and buy more before she could have her meal.

Mum did live happily in her bungalow for two and a half years; then she needed more care than I could give, she made one more move, into a nursing home. She was settled there, gaining weight from being able to eat in company. She died two and a half years later at the age of 88.

We were lucky mum was pleasant in her dementia, all who cared for her said she was a pleasure, always remembering her, 'please and thank you's.' and she was grateful for what they did for her.

End

Jason Ginnely with another poem about the curse that effects many with depression, the enemy of overthinking

Believing.

You look deep in thought... Are you listening?

I'm thinking, pondering, questioning.

What are you contemplating?

Everything that's happening and I'm experiencing.

Is it helping?

Not really, it's troubling,

In what way?

Hiding, sheltering, dwelling and not rebuilding,

just...just preserving.

Can I help you?

How, I don't really know what I'm feeling?

By calming, soothing, nurturing and enriching.

I don't know if I'm deserving,

I'm changing, disappearing, vanishing...

I can't work out when I stopped flying and just focused on floating.

You need to stop punishing you.

It's life, it's colouring your enlightening.

Some things are deceiving and distorting your developing.

You've stopped receiving encouraging,

You're travelling without moving,

But it doesn't need to be defining,

perhaps...

perhaps, what?

You need a jolt of momentary lightning,

That will provide the sparking to,

Re-energising your existing.

To just stop breathing and start living, again.

Are you willing?

I don't know, maybe...Yes,

What do I need to be doing?

Start talking, listening, trying,

Searching, playing, exploring,

And keep checking what you're mirroring in others,

Reflecting on what's troubling, triggering and hurting you

And be kind to yourself and work on how to stop it continuing.

How?

Be loving and caring to yourself,

How?

By believing...by Believing

Frank Varley again, with a poem about our apposable digit…I'm all fingers myself.

Thumbs

It's a minefield

Scrolling on your phone

You glide your thumb down the screen

Moving further down is the action you mean

But you touch too hard

You're of that age

Aaargh no!

You've liked a breastfeeding page.

CeCe Hemmings

CeCe Hemmings is one half of electronic/alternative duo Hemmingway, who have recently caught the attention of BBC Introducing, BBC London and Tom Robinson (BBC 6). Her career as a singer/songwriter/producer has spanned almost 30 years, working alongside notable artists such as The Shamen, The Prodigy, Moby and D:Ream. As well as her passion for writing lyrics, she is also in the process of editing her debut novel, aiming for publication in 2019.

Her background is Anglo Indian, which has led to having life experiences that have influenced her work.

CeCe currently lives in Essex with her children.

This is a fantastic emotional piece. Using a first person's point of view increases the impact of the overall message.

Black and Blue

You put me on a pedestal,

Shoot me up into the sky,

Slowly seep into my veins,

Get me addicted to your high,

When I come crashing down,

Mind twisted and bent,

I slowly start to wonder why,

Don't feel like it's by accident.

Now I am lost, I can't survive,

How did I get here?

Can't find my way back to the light.

My heart, my soul, my spirit's

Beaten black and blue,

Since when did this become a way of saying

"I love you"

What am I going to do?

You give with one hand, then you take,

Feel like I'm spinning round and round,

The voice inside my head is yours,

No matter how I try to drown it out,

The bruises that you leave on me,

They go far beyond the skin,

My body looks untouched, unharmed,

Can't see the damage done within.

My heart, my soul, my spirits beaten

Black and blue,

What am I going to do?

Halima Mayat has been writing since 13. She runs a monthly women's poetry group at Westgate Studios, Wakefield. Her poetry is mainly on personal issues, she suffers from bipolar & eating disorders.

This is a re-imagining of the old Little Red Riding Hood tale, it reflects Halima's condition and is a lovely little metaphor.

Subversive

Once upon a time, Little red riding hood's mum, gave her a basket of apples,

told her to take them to her granny but not to go to the deep, dark, dangerous forest.

So, after taking her morning dosage of anti-depressant, off she went.

Halfway through her walk, she got hungry, so she munched & crunched her way through 3 apples.

She was sure her granny wouldn't mind her eating 3 apples.

After, about 10 minutes, she got hungry, again...

So, she munched & crunched her way through 3 more apples.

At this rate, she was going to get her to grannies with no apples.

So, she decided to go through the deep, dark, dangerous forest.

She encountered a wolf, she looked at the wolf, with hungry eyes & said 'I am so hungry,

I could gobble you up'.

The wolf looked at the hunger in her eyes & fled.

Her insatiable appetite from her anti-depressant were a blessing for once!

END

This is Jonathan Terranova. Jonathan is a poet from Carlisle, based in Kent. He was featured by Gigwise as one of eight contemporary poets to challenge the art form. His first collection 'Longing For More' was released February this year and he's currently working on his first novel.

Jonathan's writing deals with personal loss, both familial and romantic.

Jonathan's main influences are Thomas Hardy, Lucia Berlin, Fyodor Dostoevsky and John Fante

This is a great piece and strikes a chord within myself. Sometimes sleep seems the only way to escape omnipresent depression.

Sleep

Some days I want to leave the world behind

I place my head on the pillow and escape

You can't upset anyone when you're asleep

For months now I've adopted this state

I work hard in the week and drink myself dumb

get a day off and hide from the sun.

If it's a good day, I'll shower and read

but literature is not a fix for grief

and the characters are too much like the past

a place from which I bleed.

Goodbye glorious day

I pray when I awake

That I'll be ok again.

This is Anne Rhodes again with a poem putting our fears and problems into perspective,

ESCAPE

Escape – that's all folk seem to need, to do.

Compared to some, our problems are so small.

Unhappiness or heartache makes us cry.

The funny bits of life can pass us by.

A stubbed toe, a broken arm or finger,

The misery brought on by loneliness.

All these, though large in our own lives as such

Are merely our own emotional crutch?

Are naught, compared to those who flee from fear,

From death or bombs or now from burning homes

A lifetime spent without acknowledgement

Now the need for swift escape is rampant.

Their houses and their property are gone

Frail or babes in arms are carried some way

Escape from fear their only driving force

From cruel villains who have no remorse.

Generations pass still unaccepted

They did not ask to be ignored or shunned

They did not ask for such strong dismissal

Indeed, is such cruel treatment lawful?

Thousands and thousands collapse where they're told

A banking, a muddy field which gets worse

The more arrive to churn its wat'ry sludge.

Too many to stay so onwards they trudge.

No-one would flee, yet bringing so little -

Walking for frightening mile upon mile

Reaching out for the world to succor them

In their time of need, and their fear to stem.

Our problems shrink to naught when thus compared

Our lives not in the same danger as theirs.

Their poor lives seem worse, the deeper one delves -

We only try to escape from ourselves.

Catherine Whittaker

Cathy has a sequence of 15 poems published in *Quintet*, Cinnamon Press. Her poems have also appeared in *Under the Radar, Prole, The Interpreters House, Envoi, Orbis, Ink Sweat and Tears, Southlight, Obsessed with Pipework, The Magnolia Review, Mslexia*, and other magazines. She was shortlisted for the *Bridport Prize* and won the *Southport Writers Competition*. Most recently her poems have been published in *#Me Too A Women's Poetry anthology* edited by Debra Alma and in *'Please Hear What I'm Not Saying'* edited by Isabelle Kenyon.

This is a well written poem explaining how anxiety can make us feel.

Anxiety

On the way to work it starts to snow
my brain begins its click and snap
I'm going to be late, going to be late,
what can I do? How can I get through?

My brain starts its click and snap
the engine sparks, the spikes turn
what can I do? how can I get through?
It never ends this litany of catastrophe.

The engine sparks, the spikes turn
I can't sleep, I can't breathe,
it never ends this litany of catastrophe,
prayer, meditation, talk, don't work.

I can't sleep I can't breathe
strapped to a wheel that I can't get off,
prayer, meditation, talk, don't work.
It won't stop, it won't ever stop.

Strapped to a wheel, I can't get off
I'm going to be late, I'm going to be late,
it won't stop, it won't ever stop.
On the way to work it starts to snow.

This is Nick Foulds in his own words…

I started writing poetry when me Mum died and I wanted to put in words what she meant to me, it sort of escalated from there..... Into music, left wing politics, disability rights (got a visually impaired son) theatre, sport, normal stuff you'd associate with a working class lad

This poem is about a mate who'd split with his partner and was trying to come to terms with all the stuff that entails, and reflecting on life in general.

Traded Places

Traded places
now stands apart
didn't hurt no one
didn't even start

It's life lad, don't be sad
Think of what you should've had
One day son it'll make you cry
Optimism, replaced with a sigh

Played the game, used your rules
Intelligence?
Not in our schools

Stand up straight
Keep in line
Do as you're told
you'll be just fine

I did as you said
and asked for nowt
managed to keep
Myself afloat

Toiled a lifetime
to earn a crust
Ambitions blown away
Like the dust

Like a mayfly
Short and sweet
Week, weekend Slow forward
and repeat

Chris Sutton is a mental health advocate, lead officer for the Healthy Minds staff network at Leeds City Council, host of the Mental Conversations podcast and wannabe children's author! Chris is committed to helping others improve their positive mental health and cites humour and honesty as the cornerstones of his approach.

Here is a fantastic funny fable about a little mouse and her adventures. Are we sitting comfortably? Good, then Chris will begin…

Dimple Scurry's Quest for the Enlighten Mint

This is the tale of Dimple Scurry,
A little mouse but one who likes to worry,
An exciting journey fraught with dangers,
An adventure filled quest meeting new friends and strangers,
Where a misplaced toe could see you fall into a bog,
And leave you as sad as a downward facing dog!

We find our little heroine staring in the mirror,
With sadness in her eyes hoping life will look much clearer,
If she focusses a little more and tries to raise a smile,
If only she could remember what to do… it's been a while!
Eventually she gives up and decides to leave the house,
She cuts such a lonely figure for such a lovely little mouse.

Dimple takes a full breath in then gives a slow exhale,
She's brushed her little teeth and polished up her long pink tail,
She steps out of the hollow of the oak tree she calls home,
"Why am I so sad?" she thinks, as she sets out to roam,
Through Beestone Woods she scurries trying not to come a cropper,
Dodging woodland trips and hazards on her way to see Grasshopper.

Fallen leaves create a multi-coloured carpet on the ground,
And Dimple's tiny footsteps make a crispy crunchy sound,
The shedding trees from one perspective could seem to be approaching
death,
Or a hibernating wonderland ready for spring's awakening breath,
Dimple likes to kick the leaves as this can help avoid attacks,
They swirl in circles in the autumn breeze and cover up her tracks.

Dimple scurries over roots as falling leaves they keep on dancing,
"It won't be long", she thinks "'til we see snow with winter soon advancing",
She scampers up a fallen branch to check the view from somewhere higher,
In this dappled sunlight some leaves look like they could be on fire,

Even in her sadness Dimple's touched by nature's grace,
As the warmth of sunlight dances through the trees to kiss her face.

Few flowers inhabit the woods at present as the colder air it settles,
Except for Snowdrops, Pussy Willows, it's more a time for nettles than petals,
The colours are still jaw dropping, leaves of orange and brown and red,
Big or small, wide or narrow, just right to make a comfy mousy bed.
And if you're searching food right now you could fill up your stocks and hampers,
As there are berries sweet or bitter but on our Dimple scampers.

There's a chirruping, scratching, whaling noise that's drifting from the grass,
And if Dimple wasn't sad she'd have to stifle back a laugh,
When a grasshopper rubs its legs together that's the way it sings,
But this strange noise comes from Hopper as she manicures her wings!!
A picture-perfect beauty in the grasshoppering world,
Even her perfect hoppy grassy eyelashes are curled.

Dimple takes a seat and tries to remain calm,
When Hopper is finally ready Dimple blurts out with alarm,
"What do I have to do to find some happiness in the end?"
Dimple takes a seat and waits to hear the wise words from her friend.
Hopper checks her lashes twice and says "It's hard to tell....
You must go and see the woodland mystic firefly Isabelle."

"There will be danger on the way" says Hopper, "You must be the judge.
If finding happiness is worth the risk of crossing paths with Smudge,
He's suspicious, crazed and bonkers and since he lost his marbles,
He talks a load of nonsense and at worst he simply garbles,
If he hears you're seeking happiness it might make him quite mad,
And he'll make it his sole mission to ensure you remain sad."

When it comes to Smudge, Hopper is right in her description,
He is marbleless and bonkers, quite an accurate depiction.
Smudge is big and winged and white and at first sight you'd see a swan,
The only trouble - if you ask he'd say he most certainly isn't one,

As in Smudge's mind he does like swans in fact he thinks they're regal,
But in his imagination, he soars above the earth - he is an eagle!

Smudge waddles around Beestone Woods like he owns the place,
He puckers up his bill to make a beak like eagle face,
Eagles have great talons for climbing; Smudge's are webbed and slippy,
He wears especially sticky gloves upon his feet to make them grippy,
Which makes him quite a funny sight when he's climbing up a tree,
Sending leaves and feathers everywhere and squawking angrily.

So, what's his story you may ask, why would he wish Dimple to fail?
The truth is Smudge's quest for happiness was a sad, depressing tale,
As although legend will have it, Smudge did in fact come close,
His failure and loss of marbles made him suspicious, paranoid and morose,
Which means he won't want others to succeed and he wouldn't think twice,
About ending Dimple Scurry's dreams and remember…. eagles…. they eat
mice!

As we return to Dimple there's a little change upon her face,
She's looking purposeful, determined seeking out Isabelle's place.
The mystic firefly, a legend living in the wood's dark caves,
Surely, she can guide our Dimple towards the happiness she craves,
There's an eerie quiet, a whispy fog and nerves as she approaches,
Trying to ignore the candle lit skeletons of dead cockroaches.

Brushing through the cobwebs of the front door, Dimple's brave,
As summoning her courage, she enters the dark and dingy cave,
There is little there to stop her and no need for her to fright,
As she scurries forwards on towards the nearing twinkling light,
"Have I reached my destination?" Dimple thinks, it's hard to tell
Can the vision she now sees be legendary Isabelle?

The oldest firefly that ever lived, her light now only flickers,
Leaning on a match and upon her head, a pair of spotty knickers,
Isabelle floats forwards, blinks her eyes and cleans her ears,
Just making sure this sight is real, she hasn't left the cave for years,

Now she ponders this brave little mouse whose eyes give her away,
She sees sadness and self-doubt, she's lost the will to laugh and play.

"Step forward child" croaks Isabelle, her voice so underused,
Dimple obeys and blinking twice is still somewhat confused,
"I sense a journey" mutters Isabelle, "yes, there's something which you seek,
Something magical to bring a smile between those dimply cheeks,
"To succeed my friend, I'll tell you now you must become a warrior,
To find some happiness, in truth, you must reverse your worrier."

Isabelle continues "child now choose, of life's roads which you'll take....
You have begun the greatest journey one can ever wish to make,
I will do my best to tell you straight or you can try to take the hint,
To find happiness you must go in search of the Enlighten Mint,
Now where to find such treasure is what I'm sure you want to know,
Well strange as it sounds I'll speak the truth, there's one place you must go,

To find the Enlighten Mint you must search for the lightening trees,
Just look atop the tallest one where you will find the can of peas!!!
It's important that you focus, to Drishti Point go quick, make haste,
That's the best place to cross the river, you haven't a second to waste",
There's a crash of sound and a flash of light and Isabelle is gone,
With this final odd instruction, Dimple turns and starts to run.

Through the dust she hears a voice "contentment comes in different ways,
............if you remember nothing else you must ensure you hold your gaze,
Find the can of peas and look inside and you'll find it through the haze,
It's important you remember child, ensure you hold your gaze........."

In Dimple's haste to leave the eerie cave she doesn't see,
The madly flapping sticky footed Smudge up in a tree,
He has heard the conversation between the mouse and firefly,
And has begun already plotting how to make poor Dimple cry!
With eagle minded focus Smudge now launches into flight,
Quite forgetting he's a swan he's really such a funny sight,

Flapping head first into bramble bushes thick with barbs and spikes,
Not exactly something this eagle thinking swan particularly likes,
It's with a red embarrassed angry face that Smudge, he now emerges,

"I will stop that little rodent finding happiness" he urges,
"To Drishti Point I'll soar above the trees and formulate a plan,
To keep that mouse in misery in any way I can".

Scurry by name and scurry by nature as this is what Dimple now does,
With her focus now firmly on Drishti Point, the excitement is starting to buzz,
As Drishti appears in the distance the strange misty scene can't escape her,
The Point comes into view but only just as its hazy and clouded with vapour,
Dimple approaches with caution and then lets out a sigh of relief,
"Alright Dimple" comes the greeting from Lizzie the lizard through vapour filled teeth.

A strange little lizard is Lizzie and she is small with cute little features,
And a marvelous smile and twinkly eyes, really one of the friendliest creatures,
To inhabit the woods and a good friend for Dimple to find at this point of this magical tale,
As she's bound to be helpful despite the odd quirk that she emits a vaporous trail,
It is maybe because she's a lizard and spends much of her time in the water,
Before sunbathing, which seems to cause the great steam as a shield like her old mummy taught her!

"Have I made Drishti Point" questions Dimple, "is this the best place to cross?"
"Yes of course" replies Lizzie, "Just make sure you watch out for the boss.
Fallen Tree Crossing is just over there but so is a scorpion and it may sound absurd,
His name is Nama and he's not very nice to those who don't know the password.
Well you seem in a hurry so off you trot" Lizzie says peering out through the mist,
And as Dimple looks back at her green little friend she's performing a low spinal twist.

The sound of the thunderous river is the next thing for Dimple to hear,
As she shudders and gulps and attempts to control the rising uncomfortable
fear,

For though our little hero has many fine skills even if her confidence was
brimming,
There's one thing she's never quite mastered and that's the art of swimming,
But on she pushes focused and brave trying to be fearful of nothing,
As now into view comes the next obstacle of traversing Fallen Tree Crossing.

On the opposite bank with a grin on his face we find Smudge looking smug
and content,
As he watches the mouse he can't help but feel her adventure is about to end,
"When she comes face to face with Nama" he thinks, "she'll surely be
stopped in her tracks,
If she can't make the payment or say the password, I'll enjoy watching when
he attacks."
Quite forgetting his lack of good balance, Smudge now slips and falls in with
a splash,
And is swept downstream, squawking and flapping again, and lucky his head
didn't crash.

Dimple stops short of the fallen tree and takes deep breath to compose,
Then inches forwards slowly her heart pounding and twitching her nose,
The crossing is wide Dimple thinks to herself "this should be easy for me,
Just don't look down, don't look up and remember it's just a tree"
But as she puts her first toe onto the tree there's a flash of black,
And when Dimple next opens her eyes she finds she is lying on her back.

The clouds are racing across the sky at the same speed that her heart is
pumping,
She scurries back onto all fours and watches this fearsome creature jumping.
Nama the bearded black scorpion paces in front of her face,
And he doesn't look best pleased to see her, trespassing in scorpion's space.
He fixes his gaze on poor Dimple, the gaze quickly turns into a stare,
Strangely wobbling around Dimple thinks right away that perhaps she
shouldn't be there.

Nama clasps hold of a small little rail that he's clearly installed on the tree,
To help him with balancing issues, so he can remain still and can be,

The dangerous looking guardian of who crosses to the other side,
Of the crashing water below them, racing at quite a pace, deep and wide.
"What is the password?" he bellows, as he readies himself to strike

"Only I have the power to let you through, I can stop whoever I like"

Dimple steps back and with fear in her voice starts to tremble and squeaks "I
don't know.
But please let me through. To continue my quest, this is the place I must go."
"I'll give you one more chance" says Nama, his voice is low and strong,
"Or you better start running or guessing" he says, "but believe me – do not
get it wrong!"
Dimple thinks for a moment, there's no option but having a guess,
She has to cross the river, or her life with remain in this mess.

"Is it 'Happy'", guesses Dimple. She holds her breath and takes a step back,
But Nama erupts and ready's his pincers, a sure sign he's about to attack,
Dimple can't move for a second as she's paralysed with fear,
And Nama's moving closer, in fact now he's incredibly near,
There's a flash of red fur and a shout she can't hear and Dimple's sent
tumbling away,
Then the words are repeated sharp, loud and clear "Nama stay....Nama
stay....Nama stay"

When Dimple regains her senses, she's held in a warm, safe embrace,
As she focusses her attention she recognises a familiar face,
Soft brown eyes filled up with kindness and a wonky uneven smile,
"Hello Conker" Dimple says, "How are you? It's been a while."
"I'm not bad" comes Conker's quick reply, "But what are you doing round
here?
Don't you know the password" he says, although the answer to that is quite
clear.

"For future reference, Dimple. When you're crossing there's one thing to say,
It really is quite simple, just remember to shout: Nama stay.......Nama
stay.......Nama stay!!!
"Where are you off to anyway? You're a long way from home you know"
"I'm looking for the lightening trees. I don't suppose you know where to go?"
"Well as it happens, yes, I do, I'd be happy to give you a hint
I don't suppose you're off in search of a can of peas and the enlighten mint?"

"How did you know that?" says Dimple, "Have you found it, can you show it
to me"

"You have to find it all by yourself" says Conker, "that's the way it must be,
I will tell you this, you are on the right track" Conker says as he looks at her
face,
I can see from your eyes that an adventurous ride is the perfect starting place,
You continue your path and remember these words. Ensure you hold your
gaze,
Look inside and remember Dimple, ensure you hold your
gaze..................."

Even Nama starts to wave when the friends say their goodbyes,
As Dimple scurries on, her hopes are starting now to rise,
If she continues this path she thinks "I might just make it, I feel great"
Her self-belief is growing quickly as she starts to contemplate,
"The possibilities of finishing my quest" she starts to smile
" I can do it, I feel strong…. I haven't felt this for a while!"

The sound of water starts to fade then disappears as Dimple flees,
As per Conker's clear directions of how to find the Lightening Trees,
The sun is shining brightly making the dew sparkle and glow,
Has Dimple found the one true path which will see her happiness grow?
She scurries quickly through the great pasture, where amid the tall green grass,
The fabled trees come into view "I'm nearly there" she thinks, "at last!"

The final steps to reach the Lightening Trees become so wet and boggy,
That by the time she reaches them Dimples fur is getting soggy,
But with brave determination the water shakes off with a shudder,
Now which tree to choose the problem as they all look like each other,
Dimple glances left and glances right and tries hard to decide,
Then eventually chooses one with scratchy paw prints on its side.

She starts the climb with butterflies inside, her heart begins to pound,
As she reaches half way up the wind around her ears is now the only sound,
Daring to look down's a big mistake highlighting her exposure,
She decides to stop and take a break and gather her composure,

One wrong move from me now I'll end up face down in that bog,
Dimple focusses her eyes and is that…. yes…. she sees a frog!

Unbeknown to Dimple, Smudge too is inhabiting this tree,
"Someone has to stop her now" he says out loud, "it must be me!"
But he misjudges as he launches from the branch he perches on,
And as Dimple looks down from on high she sees downward facing swan!
Flapping wildly once again Smudge flies away and disappears,
Whilst trying to clean the mud out of his beak, his nose and ears!

Approaching now with caution, Dimple moves towards the frog she's seen,
Standing on one leg, her eyes closed she is focused, balanced and green,
Dimple coughs to draw attention and the frog opens one eye,
Loses balance and starts to wobble, quite precarious up this high,
"Hello" comes the croaky friendly voice, "My name is Tiffany"
Are you seeking something special, maybe a life changing epiphany?"

"I have come to find the Enlighten Mint" says Dimple, "It's inside a can of
peas,
Somewhere up high around here, I'm told it's in the Lightening Trees"
Tiffany gives a chuckle and asks "Who told you all that?
Was it Isabelle the firefly, you know she's as crazy as a bat!
Don't you think that maybe what she meant was in the canopy?
That's the only thing that makes sense at all if you're asking me"

Dimple thinks for a second then she nods that perhaps that does make sense,
"But either way I must keep climbing" the excitement is growing intense,
"You are very brave" says Tiffany, "there's a warrior in you"
I wish you luck my friend, after all, I'd like to be a warrior too!"
The new acquainted friends say their goodbyes and Dimple scurries higher,
Climbing fearlessly, determined inside her belly she feels fire.

After what feels like forever Dimple makes it to the top,
Of the tallest of the Lightening Trees where now she can finally stop.

She looks around about her, now confused - what does she seek?
Then inside her mind she recalls Isabelle's words begin to speak,

She remembers what the firefly said "contentment comes in different ways,
............if you remember nothing else you must ensure you hold your gaze"

Dimple takes a deep breath in then lets fate decide which way she faces,
Trust in the strength she's shown to get here and in destiny she places,
From this high up Dimple can see across Beestone Woods that now seems
like a woodland maze,
Then she sees it.... Drishti Point below, she focusses, then holds her gaze,
After what could be several hours Dimple's mind has become quite clear,
Then as her eyes open slightly wider there's a sparkling object that's quite
near.

Dimples heart is in her mouth now as she regains her full attention,
And scampers towards the shining light, she can barely stand the tension,
Then she sees it in full glory, unquestionably a can of peas!
But as Dimple looks inside, her heart sinks and she falls down to her knees.
For there's not much to find within it and there's no Enlighten Mint,
Just a couple of dusty old marbles, Dimples eyes start to squint.

"Remember what you've been told" she thinks once again, as the words she
replays,
"If I remember nothing else, I must ensure I hold my gaze................"
Dimple lets the marbles roll out into her palm then peers inside again,
She lets her eyes relax yet focusses and at once feels a release of the pain,
That's she's felt for such a long time, within minutes it's becoming clear,
What has held her back for all this time has been simply based on fear.

Holding her gaze and peering inside Dimples mind starts to make a
correction,
As she realises that what is deep inside the can is simply her reflection,
Then it dawns on her all that Isabelle and Conker were suggesting with pride,
Was that the enlightenment we seek is simply what we have inside,
It is not a destination or somewhere we must travel to find,
It's the journey that we take in our body, soul and mind!

Dimple puts the can back where she found it and turns to leave,

Then looks down at the marbles and with a smile begins to breath,
A full and deep breathe filled with hope and renewed belief that life will be,
Now changing for the better and forever it's clear to see,
"I think maybe I'll go home now" Dimple thinks, as she descends,
And on top of this adventure I've made some wonderful new friends.

Dimple smiles and waves at Tiffany the Tree Frog as on she scurries,
Then on to Fallen Tree Crossing, now with the password she has no worries,
But just as she approaches, there's a flash of white before her eyes,
And she's knocked into the river, "I can't swim" our Dimple cries,
Then the world goes dark again, her eyes are closed, and all is still,
When she comes to the only thing she can see is a giant orange bill.

There's a crazed look in the eyes of Smudge as he's peering down at Dimple,
Filled with anger, fear and confusion it seems his aim's quite simple,
It's to end the journey of our heroine once and for all,
But as he goes to flip her in the air Dimple opens her paw and lets the marbles fall,
Smudge's eagle face is quite a picture as he starts to realise,
The magnitude of what he now can see before his eyes.

"I found your marbles" squeaks Dimple Scurry, as she holds them up to see,
"I thought maybe you'd like them back, I hope that wasn't wrong of me?"
Smudge pushes his bill forwards and places the marbles in his pouch one by one,
And as he does so his face changes from a squinty eagle to that of a beautiful swan,
He glides across the water and he places Dimple on one of the river banks,
Then turns around and bows his head to show respect and swan like thanks.

"I'm not an eagle" says Smudge, "that's right, look at me, I'm a swan"
And of all the things I know there's one truly important one,

Shall I tell you now my friend the difference between eagles and swans I'll tell you twice?"

Dimple exhales with relief as Smudge continues "Swans……. they don't eat mice!"
"So, did you find the Enlighten Mint" say Smudge, "did you find the can of peas?"
"That's a journey you must take yourself" says Dimple "head towards the Lightening Trees"

"Is there just one route to find my happiness" says Smudge "or are there many different ways"
Dimple smiles at her new friend; she pats his wing and simply says,
"When you find the can of peas Smudge, just remember contentment comes in different ways,
…………………….if you remember nothing else you must ensure you hold your gaze!!!!"

THE END

Set an intention to always live life joyfully,
To laugh often,
To love well,
To serve others greatly,
And to be more love.

Many blessings,

Namaste

For Lucy and the Vinyasa Flow Riders. My inspiration, my laughter and my breath!

This is David Bradshaw, in his own words:

Poet, short story writer, and the first Mother Superior to unicycle up Mount Everest, David Bradshaw is two of these things, and sometimes more.

David has suffered from depression and anxiety for many years, yet he has a master's degree in English Literature from Leeds University, a Bachelor of Arts degree in English and Film, and a bronze swimming certificate.

David likes Pina Colladas and taking walks in the rain, he also hopes to bring about world peace...somehow! He lives in Leeds, West Yorkshire, with just a pencil, a notepad, and his considerable genius! His birth-sign is 'Slippery When Wet', and his favourite colour is Tuesday.

Here's a brilliant, darkly comic poem

Unstable Brian

Unstable Brian's

Not a man to rely on,

As he has other things in his head.

You'd be shocked and surprised

By the gleam in his eyes,

As he sharpens his axe in the shed.

He's an upstanding pillar

For a serial killer,

With apparently good mental health.

And the neighbors, when asked

Of the man and his past,

Say he's, "Quiet. Keeps himself to himself".

He may stalk, lure and kill

But he still pays the bills,

And he once had some people to stay.

They were all warmly greeted

And the room plastic sheeted,

In case of arterial spray.

Not the cleanest of hobbies

But he's skilled with the bodies,

And he makes sure they're wrapped up with care.

For he's terribly clean

And quite calm and serene,

As he piles them up under the stairs.

Brian used to be married

But so constantly harried,

That he found it a nightmare to please her.

So instead of divorce

He dispelled all remorse,

And now bits of her live in the freezer.

He's amazingly placid

While a bath full of acid,

Upstairs eats a victim to nothing.

Brian's fun never ends

Though it's hard to make friends,

And takes hours of mounting and stuffing.

Danielle Tait is a single mother from Bridlington

This a beautifully sad poem about the contemplation of taking one's own life.

Just one more
As she sparks up her last cigarette
I'm fine
As she hides her last regret
Another shot
As she falls to the floor
Sharpens the blade
Cries for help once more
Life's what you make it
So, pick yourself up
Try losing yourself in a book
One life to live
Friends by your side
So, suck it up
And swallow your pride
It's okay to hurt
It's okay to cry
Only you can make it better
Before you say goodbye
Time is borrowed
Your hearts the key
It takes loving yourself
To live happily

This is Naomi Wang, in her own words;

Got the audition for Disney in 1992, playing electric violin and mandolin, so we moved to Paris for 4 years. Appearing in 7 shows a day or night, playing to over 80,000 people a week, plus film, TV & recording so high exposure.

On return to London, discovered that I wasn't an 'idiot' or 'backwards' by shockingly, getting a place at Brunel University in 1997-2000 getting a 2.1 Hons degree in Music & Performing Arts. As a mature student obviously.

Then had two teaching contracts in two state special schools to teach music, dance and drama from the curriculum for 4 days a week, touring for the other 3 days with my now ex-husband with our band, playing festivals – (Glastonbury x2), & gigs all over UK & Europe, sometimes with an agent, plus recording about 7 cds/albums & air play here and worldwide.

Finally, last year in 2017 at the Arvon Centre, Yorkshire, I did a week-long Life Writing course which kick started my story, so here's a small part of it!

It's NOT a poor me story, more about how to survive and succeed no matter what's happened in the past, but I have worked hard to build myself into a person, when I could've easily just gone under. But I'm feisty fortunately & have humility & insight, hopefully intelligent as I've recently discovered. Working on modesty. The good thing about being a non-person, is that you can completely build yourself into the sort of person you really want to be. I started with a blank sheet. Use your artistic license. Building from the bits of others who've touched my life, which I respect, love, admire & desire, and I'm always curious.

Thank You for reading my chapter!

Here is a harrowing autobiographical piece. **NOTE** this work contains phrases and issues that some people may find upsetting.

BIRD OF PASSAGE

Two messages on the answerphone:

1. "Bonjour, it's your stage manager here from Disneyland Paris, you've got the audition, the contracts in the post"

2. You'd killed yourself on Christmas Day 1991.

You went mad so many times I lost count. Your breakdowns increased in frequency, got closer together, until eventually, they all joined up and you never recovered. Not that you'd ever properly recovered before....

Often, you were locked away in cells in mental institutions like Wimbledon, Longrove Epsom or.... I think that was where you had ECT...or was it Wimbledon. You hated ECT. You said it made you forget things. Like our names, your four children's names.

We never ever bonded. You rejected me from birth. Possibly as you weren't yet married to Kurt David Wang from Vienna, Austria when you conceived me.

My Great Aunt Seraphina, or Aunty Finni, and Uncle Emil also from Vienna who'd both escaped from concentration camps, (And there lies another story) came to live in Maida Vale, London, and became my surrogate grandparents. They taught me what love could be.

You chose to 'forget' to take your medication when they 'let you out'. So, you went back into your dark, crazy, cruel, torturing, distorted, spiteful, lying (you were so good at lying) hateful, vicious, manic depressive, psychotic, hyper-manic, schizophrenic, bi-polar self. Self.

Are you still a self with all that to bear? Where was your Self? You lost it years ago, after you conceived me. Or maybe, if true as you lied so much, it was when your Russian father sexually abused you...

Aunty Finni told me that you wanted an abortion when you realised you were going to have me. Helpful to know this? YES. It explained why you physically, intellectually, emotionally and socially ABUSED ME. EVERY DAY OF MY LIFE. You didn't want me inside you...

Your doctor told you not to have any more children after my next brother, 8 years after me. But he was a boy........and you desperately wanted a boy as your first child, you made that perfectly clear. He was the only planned child. And it shows to this day, a very balanced, calm, kind brother who lives in Cape Town with his wife and 2 grown up daughters, very far away from you. But he suffered too, from your madness.

Why did you keep it such a secret that you had me taken away and fostered for months after I was born. I found out. But I never found out the truth, that one of my legs got broken as a baby. A secret, secret. You alluded to this 'event' on several occasions...but never told me what really happened.

You were SO CRUEL AND TORTUOUS. Some days, when you ran a bath for me when I was 2, 3, 4, 5 ...you'd put me in such fucking hot baths and left me there till I screamed to be taken out.

You did this intentionally to PUNISH me, you said "You're a horrible, nasty little brat, just wait till your father gets home"

The bright red mark's of the burning water on my little legs drew a line across my bottom and thighs until you eventually took me out and 'dried' me SO roughly, you punished me. You'd 'wash' my front bottom with soap that'd sting me so much I could hardly walk or go to the toilet. The pain was...well, what you took pleasure from, exactly what you intended.

Do you remember beating me daily? Viciously. Violently. And saying, "And this is for the one you didn't get yesterday so you're getting double and the BIGGEST THRASHING YOU'VE EVER HAD IN YOUR LIFE" and lay into me slapping hitting, baring teeth, god you were so ugly, your adult strength rammed my head into the bedroom walls. You relentlessly punched, kicked and hit me, it just went on and on. "You're an idiot, you're backward" ....and I believed you.... well you do if someone tells you that every day of your life.

Do you remember saying threateningly "If you don't behave I'll pull your knickers down in the street and give you such a hiding so that everyone can see what a naughty brat you are"

And you did. Daily... in Putney High St. Or more often behind closed doors in the flat, I used to think in dread, "Wonder when you'll 'do it' today".

You know what? Everyone just walked past ignoring me while you unleashed your spiteful, hateful anger on my bottom, head, anywhere you could reach my body. And everyone ignored you too...???. That was then, in the 1950's, now it would called Public Humiliation...and you'd be in prison for child abuse. Every day I wanted to kill myself and did try by holding my breath while lying on a rug on the floor next to my bed, but it didn't work!

Much later, Lilian C, the 'family' friend who found your drowned body, told me "I always suspected what was going on, but you just didn't or couldn't interfere in those days" and profoundly apologised to me, which helped me through the damage much later. She would often take me home from school in Southfields with her children to her house in Wandsworth when you didn't or 'forgot' to come to collect me when I was 5 and went on the tube from East Putney to Southfields to school, often by myself.

And do you remember how I used to wait by the front door in the hall of the one bedroom flat at 49, Millbrook Court Keswick Road, Putney SW15. Didn't think you did for one minute, conveniently. I'd wait for my daddy to come home from work, just so I could show him what you'd done to me every day, the bruises and hurt. Always crying and sobbing. But he rarely did.

Pushing his own career as an articled clerk for what went on to become the most famous company of lawyers in the country, who advise parliament, the Queen, even to this day.... the world-famous company still exists....in London.

He had a very strong Austrian-German accent then, when he spoke English, which would embarrass me later, well he'd only been in London for less than 8 years when I was born, and he was my saviour, then....

Did you ever know that I wished, desperately, for a phone which could show pictures? No, thought you didn't. You are so horrible, I hate you. I am here writing as my five-year-old self. As an adult I was so stunned to see and hear that the Apple guy Steve Jobs, I think it was him invented the phone which took pictures. Why didn't I invent it when I was 4 or 5? I was totally desperate for my daddy to see, know and hear what you did to me when he wasn't there. But he didn't ever know....

Do you remember when I was 4 and 5, you made me go to bed at 5.30-6.00pm as usual with the bedroom door, tightly shut? The 'door' was not up for discussion ---------- I had to just 'Do as you're told' god I was desperate for you to die. Or me.

My animals consisting of Teddy, Rabbit and Dog were all next to me along the bed side next to the wall. Yes, I had my own bed now, just out of a cot where you'd leave me for hours all wet from my nappies.

I used to plead with you to, leave the bedroom door open "Please mummy, just a little bit? Please, Please? But you just ignored me....

...Do you remember opening the bedroom door......very...very...very slowly ....a tiny bit at a time...barely moving, so that a thin line of upside down L shaped crack of hall light ...around the door....got wider and wider ...until it opened ...enough for you to come into the room...on all fours...crawling

...with the grey ironing blanket over your head and body covering you up completely......none of you could be seen................then really, really, really slowly, you crawled across the floor towards the end of my bed? Absolutely shaking, terrified, hysterical and screaming for my daddy to come home and rescue or save me. But he never did.......

I called you the 'Harry', the boy's name I hated most. The Harry moved steadily to the end of my bed.....................by now I was really shaking and howling with fright and dread...I had got to know what was about to happen, it'd happened so many times before...

Then really, slowly I sensed the blankets & sheet at the end of my bed being opened.... I could feel ...the sensation of the blankets & sheet moving against the skin on my feet....so I curled my legs up towards my body........and then it opened enough for the Harry to put her hands inside the bed.............and start to search for my feet....to pull me down the inside of the bed.....by now my heart was pounding so hard it could've jumped out of my skin. I was suffocating under the blankets, shaking with fear...

Being hysterical and sobbing was no use, no one heard me, and I was beside myself. Still can't sleep even now. You did this to me systematically, like all the 'punishments' for being a naughty brat. I didn't even have a name. I just lived in terror every night waiting and watching for that upside-down L shape of light to appear....

A poem here from someone who wishes to remain anonymous. It's about what we witness and what we choose to see. Perhaps it's a comment on the lost and dispossessed.

Hungry Eyes

Hungry eyes

We all walk past them

Try not to notice

When their eyes are pleading

No food, no water

Not our problem

Why should we bother?

Let somebody else sort them?

It's a shame, people say

But no-one helps them

Just leave them there

It's not our problem

This is Karen Grayson in her own words:

This poem is for my best friend, Susan, who I sadly lost to suicide recently.

I haven't written any poetry since I was at school, but I just had the need to write something for this beautiful lady.

Karen Grayson, 49, Leeds

We all pick up the pen for some reason or other. In this case a beautiful sad tribute to a much-loved lost friend.

Susan

I was there that morning

I gave you a hug

I sat, and I listened

I did what I could

I could see your pain

I felt it too

But oh, my friend

If only I knew

That getting you help

Was too little too late

And that, you had already,

Decided your fate

I'm now left wishing

I'd called you that night

A text wasn't enough

To help you to fight

I tried every day

To keep you here

But you were too sad

And filled with such fear

Now you're at peace

And I do know why

But it doesn't make it easier

And it's hard not to cry

You knew that we loved you

I told you that day

I just wish I'd have known

The right words to say

To make it all better

And take the pain away

And then perhaps

You'd have decided to stay

You were my best friend

And always will be

And I can take some comfort

In knowing you're free

I will never forget

Your smile through my tears

A memory that will last

The rest of my years

With much love

Karen

This is Kerry Williamson a wonderful writer from Barnsley. Kerry is happily married with a son and is a Primary school teacher.

This is a beautifully written heart-breaking story about loss and how it affects family.

Another Cup of Tea

The room was quiet, but not too quiet. Conversation had lost its battle for life long ago. The walls used to look on when the family was being a family. It seemed like only strangers lived there now and the walls had no laughter to contain. The television was on, providing the routine sounds of normality. The television was always on. After all, you can't have awkward silences without silence. The television was an old set. Ancient. But there was no need for a new one; it was good enough for them. It showed the news daily and sport at the weekends. That was its only purpose these days. Apart from gathering dust that is. Many objects in the house gathered dust. The small Christmas tree with the bare branches was still behind the sofa in a carrier bag and it was now March. Why bother putting it back in the attic just to take it down again eleven months later? Gwen preferred to do as little as possible. She seemed to gather dust at the same rate as the television.

The armchair in front of the window was relatively new. It didn't match the sofa or the rocking chair. It didn't even match the carpet. It had been placed in its special window-blocking position to stop the light peering in. the silhouette of the chair was visible on the snooker table on the television. It didn't bother Steve Davis though, he was ahead by three frames. You could always see the chair on the screen, especially if it was a bright, sunny day. But that wasn't a regular occurrence. The first sign of sunshine forced the curtains to be closed, just in case any pleasantness tried to enter.

A sudden sound from the kitchen burst through the open door as the kettle clicked off. It must be three o'clock.

"Cup of tea?" The woman's voice seemed to sound strange and unwelcome although the three words were familiar.

"Cup of tea?" A little louder but not quite loud enough to penetrate jack's brain.

"Suit yourself."

The kitchen was dark. Gwen could see from the door that the steam from the kettle had blurred the window. She looked at it for a moment and was tempted to scribe her name with her index finger. No. it would only leave a mark that she would have to clean later. A teabag was in a cup, a small mound of sugar covering it like glistening frost. As the water was poured, the frost melted. The cup had been there for hours – since the last cup had been finished with. Finally, it got its chance to be filled. She made the tea like a robot. Six cups of tea per day, every day for the last fifty-two years. Her brain could not be bothered to work out how many that was. She wasn't quick anymore. A lot though, she thought. She had left the spoon in a little too long and she just managed to stir the tea before dropping the spoon in the sink and rubbing her newly warmed fingers. She burnt them almost every time. Six times a day for fifty-two years. How did she have any skin left?

She returned to the living room and returned to his dark glare. She had made herself a cup of tea. He had wanted one.

"Hey," he protested in his familiar deep but gentle tones. The glare was returned to him. As she turned away, she felt his eyes burn her cardigan. His hatred filtered through the woollen stitches trying to reach her heart. It never did. She never asked him if he would like a cup of tea.

*****

But at least his head was filled with happy thoughts once again. He lived for these moments. John had just left home to move into his new palace. But he never forgot where his roots were firmly planted. He was a good son. His visits were the highlights of the week. A chance to catch up on the events that had taken place for each. Father and son. Pride and joy. John was twenty-four and made his living in a stuffy office. He wore a tie to work. Jack was happy with that. Men should wear ties. You can't take a man seriously unless he's wearing a tie. That had been his mother's favourite phrase that she would use to make him look smart. John always visited after work on a Thursdays and Jack had convinced himself that today was indeed Thursday. He smiled to himself as he anticipated the familiar sound of the front door handle.

*****

Gwen finished her tea and wiped her hand across her mouth. Seeing the wetness above her cardigan cuff, she then rubbed it into the floral fabric of her skirt. It was the third day she had donned that garment. She didn't see the point of getting dolled-up to sit in the house all day. These days she tended to put as little effort as possible into everything that she did. She felt too old to make a fuss. She stood up to return the mug to the kitchen.

"Ma."

She glanced briefly at Jack before turning her back to him.

"Mother," he called again, sounding a little impatient. A slight anger was starting to simmer beneath her skin. Chewing her top lip, she started to walk towards the door. Her feet left the green carpet and stepped onto the beige linoleum. The soles of her slippers became a tapping sound as she pattered over towards the window. Taking a deep breath, she placed the mug into the steel sink alongside the lonesome teaspoon.

She could feel his presence behind her and she turned to see him standing in the kitchen doorway. His eyes were full of confusion. They had been for almost two years now. They seemed to be asking her something; he was puzzled.

"Mother," he called again.

Why should see tell him again that she is his wife, not his mother? It was nearly every day now that she had to explain to him. The disease had taken his mind and left him with only questions. She tried to stay quiet and ignore him.

"Mother?" His voice almost reaching a shout.

Her frustration overflowed and her surprisingly booming voice burst through.

"For Christ's sake Jack, I'm your wife not your bloody mother! When are you gonna realise that? Eh?"

No answer. Instead he turned to re-enter the living room, his face holding a hurt expression. She knew she shouldn't have shouted at him. Deep down she knew it wasn't his fault really. If she tried to stop herself from shouting, something inside her took over and she shouted at him anyway. She sometimes thought that she could snap him out of it, make him realise who he is, how old he is. If she yelled loud enough, he might take notice. The more she tried however, the more she realised it was no use. He was gone, and she could not get him back. Ever. She would often sit and think about the past. She had started to do it now. Her mind played back the old film of memory. They were newlyweds. She spent her days cleaning the house and then cooking the dinner while he slaved away at his important job. Five-thirty arrived at the same time as Jack did. He would enter the kitchen, put his arms around her from behind before turning her body round to place a loving kiss on her welcoming lips. He had loved her with all his heart as she had loved him. He had been a good husband. Now he spent most of his time believing that she was his mother.

*****

Jack's mother was in the kitchen. He thought again about following her in there, but he changed his mind. She would only shout at him. He couldn't understand it. She never used to shout at him for nothing. Maybe she was getting old and her patience was slipping away from her. Jack sat down in the odd armchair. It was his favourite seat and although it was quite new to the furniture collection, he much preferred it to the old, soft and comfortable settee. He paused for a second before looking down at his wrinkled hands. A signet ring of gold and onyx decorated a finger on his right hand. That was John's, but John did not know it yet. Jack had decided to give it to him as a twenty-fifth birthday present. It had been a gift to him from his own father and so it felt right to continue the tradition. He made his eyes concentrate on the back of his hand. They seemed even more crinkled than the last time he had checked. Where had these wrinkles come from? He looked as wrinkled as his mother! A quiet chuckle escaped from his throat. She would not appreciate a comment about her age, Jack realised. Life was going so quickly these days. It seemed like yesterday that John was born, and Jack was already as wrinkled as a prune. He had brought his son home from the hospital, placed him in his cot and sincerely promised him the world. Now the baby was a man. It didn't bother Jack. He still felt the same pride and love that he had always felt for his precious son. He lifted his eyes to focus on the clock. Not long to go now before John's next visit.

*****

Gwen breathed a heavy sigh before returning to the living room. Her slippers left the pattering kitchen floor and she stepped onto the silent carpet. Giving Jack a look of despair, she turned and sat back down on the settee. Just as her bottom landed, Jack rose slowly from the armchair. He turned and walked weakly to the hallway. Gwen had her back to the door, but she quickly sensed that he was climbing the stairs. The familiar creak of one of the floorboards assured her that he was almost at the top. She should follow him really. He could hurt himself. But she didn't.

A moment later, Jack returned to the living room. He carried a pair of shoes in each hand. They were his – his best black leather pair and his old gardening pair. The toes were scuffed on the gardening shoes, the laces were fraying and the colour faded. It didn't matter to Jack now because he did not do the gardening anymore. His mother wouldn't let him. He kept the shoes though, just in case he absolutely had to tend to the weeds. But there wasn't much chance of that. He walked over towards the gas fire, bent down and placed the shoes neatly side by side in front of it. He returned to his standing position and smiled proudly at the footwear. He turned to go back to the hall door and back up the stairs.

Gwen sighed to herself as she heard Jack repeating his climb. He was doing it again. For the last month he had carried out the strange ritual of lining his shoes up in the living room. Gwen would watch in amazement as the footwear was placed in front of the fire. She knew it was the illness but could not help thinking to herself that maybe he put them there for her to trip over. After all, she only seemed to shout at him these days. She could not comprehend the motive behind his bizarre routine, but she never moved them. That would only upset him and maybe confuse him even more. The creak of the stairs informed her that he was returning.

The door crept open and Jack entered. This time he held a pair of beige canvas shoes and an old pair of slippers. The beige pair was still very clean despite being a good few years old. But he did only wear them in the summer. As if like clockwork, he shuffled over to the fireplace and placed the shoes at the side of the others. Smiling to himself, he turned to make the routine journey once more. Gwen noticed that the back of the left slipper had a hole worn into it. When Jack reached the door, he paused and turned to Gwen.

"Is it Thursday today?" he had asked that question earlier.

"I've told you before Jack, it's Tuesday," his wife replied.

"I think it's Thursday. Are you sure it's not Thursday? It must be Thursday. It's Thursday," Jack muttered quickly, assuring himself.

"Fine, Jack," Gwen replied sharply. "It's Thursday." Satisfied with her answer, he continued upstairs.

Gwen realised how important Thursdays were to him. It was the day of John's visit. But she knew he would not be coming today. Jack was convinced of the opposite; he thought it was Thursday. She began to realise that today was one of those days. It happened quite often nowadays. It broke her heart, it broke his heart, but it had to be done.

Jack reappeared at the hallway door after the last instalment of his escapade. Holding a black pair in one hand and a brown pair in the other, he shuffled over to the fireplace. He slowly lowered himself to place the shoes next to the others. He took his time to make them look neat and tidy and then straightened himself. He stood over the shoes, smiling at them and feeling proud of his achievement. After a second, he moved to sit in the armchair. Gwen watched his face as he stared at the shoes. His eyes never moved. She could remember looking into those same eyes and seeing love and safety. She couldn't see that now. Jack had turned into a different person. His outer shell remained the same apart from the extra wrinkles. It was his soul, brain and personality that had been taken from them. He was empty now and Gwen still could not understand why. She realised that it was an illness, a disease, but she still had questions. Why him?

*****

Jack continued to gaze at his footwear. He liked his shoes and they looked smart when they were lined up. His mother always made him put his shoes neat and tidy. His bedroom always had to be neat and tidy. The footwear was lined up just as she had asked. If everything is in its proper place, you'll never misplace anything, she always told him if his room began to get messy. She wouldn't shout at him today.

*****

Gwen watched the television as Jack rose from the chair. He shuffled over to the fireplace to retrieve the first two pairs. Turning his back on the others, he made his way to the stairs once again. He had finished with the footwear. Now they had to be returned to their proper place in his wardrobe. It was futile, to Gwen at least. To Jack it was an important job that needed doing daily. Gwen continued to stare at the green baize on the television although she wasn't taking any notice of the game. Her mind had drifted elsewhere. She thought of her son, her only child. He had been a good son and Gwen had been proud of him. At times she would wish that he was still here, living at home. He would have been able to help her cope with her ever-changing husband. At least she would have had someone to hold a conversation with.

They could have laughed and joked. Gwen could not remember the last time she had laughed. Jack giggled to himself all the time. He did not recognise the hurt and the pain that she continually felt. He did not have the memories that she had, as he could not remember hardly any of the last twenty years. She had to keep reminding him of the cold truth. Some weeks it was every day and today was one of them.

When Jack arrived back downstairs after returning the last pair, he ambled over towards the kitchen. As he reached the door, he turned slowly to Gwen.

"Is it Thursday?"

She chose not to answer him. Instead, she glared blankly at the dusty screen.

"John will be here soon," he muttered as he walked into the kitchen. When he was out of sight, Gwen let the single tear fall down her old cheek. Her bottom lip began to quiver as she thought of her son. Her heart was heavy, and it acted as if it were in pain. Another tear formed and set off down her face. Then another, and another. She lifted her right arm and wiped her cheeks dry with her cardigan sleeve. She couldn't let Jack see her crying. Not yet. She couldn't tell him just yet.

Jack had decided to make himself a cup of tea. She had not made him one. If only he could find the bloody teabags. Where the hell were they? His eyes scanned the shelves in the pantry. Focusing on the sugar bowl, he tried to recall what the substance was. It looked like salt, but he knew that salt was kept in a small pot with a hole in the top. He knew that. Oh well, he thought, someone must have put the salt in a bowl! His eyes moved through the objects. He knew what teabags looked like; he just could not see them. After another second of searching, he lifted down a small pile of bun cases. He sighed as he turned them over with his fingers. You can't make tea with them, he thought. He returned them to their place on the shelf. His eyes then shifted back to the sugar bowl. They were next to it! An old Nescafé jar was filled with circular tea bags. He took the jar down and walked with it to the kettle. Slowly, he screwed the lid off, dropping it to the floor. His reflexes were not the same as they used to be. Lifting the lid of the kettle, he peered inside to check the water level. There was enough in there for one cup. He wasn't making her one anyway. He wiggled his long, thick fingers into the jar and pulled out three teabags, which he then plopped into the kettle. He turned his back on the appliance and sauntered back to the pantry, his left foot just scraping the edge of the jar lid, which was still lying on the linoleum. There was one space on the shelf, next to the sugar bowl. He lifted the jar and placed it carefully in the space before going back to his armchair.

Gwen lifted her head and watched Jack shuffle over to the chair. Her face was as dry as she could get it. Her eyes may have been slightly red – evidence of the tears – but he would not notice that anyway. Especially if she didn't look at him. Jack sat down, crossed his legs at the ankles and folded his arms. His eyes blank, he aimed that at the focal point of the living room. He tried to watch the snooker. He thought he recognised the man leaving over the green table, but he could not place him. He could not remember his name either. What were they doing? The cogs in his head weren't revolving very quickly today. Jack recalled holding one of those sticks himself. He used to play with Ted, his brother. You had to hit the white ball with the stick, and then the white ball would hit another ball, which would hopefully go down the hole.

Jack lifted a pointed index finger, closed his left eye and held his finger in front of his face. The man on the television disappeared behind it. He held his finger still, opened his left eye and quickly closed the right. The man was back. He switched eyes so that it was his left eye that was shut, and the man went back behind his finger. He swapped eyes again to bring the man back into view. As he continued his game, a giggle rose from deep in his chest. Gwen looked at him and could not help but notice how happy he was. Life was so simple for him. If only he knew.

*****

Jack placed his hands in his lap as his mind wandered. He remembered last Thursday, the day of John's last visit. He had walked into the living room, his face beaming.

"Hello, you two," he had said walking over to hug his mother. He was a very loving son and would hug Jack also.

"Had a good day at the office?" Jack had asked him.

"Not bad," had been the reply. Jack remembered the tie he had worn. It was checked. Lots of squares of different blues. Like his eyes. He could not stop the smile from appearing on his thin lips. He glanced at the clock and although he could not quite make out the time, he knew that John would be on his way. John had the ability to light up the room. He wasn't a big man, but his personality was. It didn't matter what kind of day Jack had endured, John would always brighten it.

*****

Gwen stood up and walked over to the television. She changed the channel for the news, turned round and returned to the settee. Her eyes met Jack's as she sat. His eyes asked a million questions although he sat in silence. She would have to talk to him soon, before he became too happy. He continued to gaze at her. The corners of her mouth lifted as her face brightened and she smiled at him. His expression did not change until Gwen's smile faded and then a grin started to form on his old face. Gwen's amused expression returned, and they sat looking at each other in silence but saying so much.

A little while later Jack emerged from his odd seat and plodded round the back of his chair. Peering through a gap in the curtains, he moaned to himself.

"Where's John?" he asked impatiently. Silence followed the question that Gwen had been dreading all day. "He should be here by now."

"Do you want a cup of tea?" Gwen enquired to change the uncomfortable subject. His head turned, and he looked at her blankly.

"Cup of tea?" Her voice was louder this time. "I'll make us a nice cup of tea."

"No," he replied abruptly.

"Do you want a biscuit then?"

"No."

"Why don't we go for a walk?" she asked.

"A walk? No."

Jack left the window and shuffled to the hallway. He went through and Gwen heard him open the front door. Jack peeped outside into the cool day. After checking up and down the street, he returned to the living room. Gwen felt the cool air around her nylon legs. As Jack sat back in the armchair, she went into the hallway to close the front door. She returned to a look of disappointment.

"John's not coming, Jack" she informed him gently. He seemed to ignore her, so she repeated herself.

"John's not coming," she announced slowly and loudly.

Rather than sitting back down, she carried on into the kitchen. She liked the idea of a biscuit. Jack followed her in there. In the pantry, she popped her finger under the biscuit barrel lid to open it. She took a rich tea and held the barrel out for Jack. He looked at Gwen, then the barrel, then back at Gwen.

"No?" she asked.

He shook his head. Gwen returned the biscuits to the gap on the shelf. Taking a deep breath, she realised it was time to break it to him. Linking arms, she walked with him back to the living room. When they reached the chair, she beckoned him to sit down and he obliged. She sat down herself on the edge of the settee and took his large but frail hand into hers.

She looked deep into his eyes and felt her heart sink.

"Jack," she started, slowly but firmly. "Now listen to me. John's not coming, you know that. Can't you remember what happened to him?"

His gaze changed direction and he looked towards the fireplace as he studied with what was left of his fading memory.

"Look at me" Gwen demanded gently. His eyes returned to hers. And then she said the sentence she had said so many times.

"Jack, John's dead. Can't you remember? He died twenty years ago." Each time she told him was harder than the last. Why couldn't he just remember? She looked into his eyes and felt his heart break. His face was full of both terror and sadness and the tears began to well.

"No," he whispered.

"Yes. I'm so sorry Jack." And as she finished her sentence, his tears fell freely. Gwen rose to put her arms lovingly around his broad shoulders. She hated these moments but there was nothing she could do. The wretched illness had taken away the one memory she wished he still had. She wished he remembered in the same way that she did. At least then she wouldn't have to break his heart every other day.

Jack cried for his precious son as though it was only yesterday that he had been taken from him. And as Gwen held him to try to ease the pain and the tears, she realised she may have to do it all again tomorrow.

END

Here is Krissie Dee Murray again with another poem about the sadness of suicide.

Different

I wait but no one shows
it happens every day
all I want is someone to hear
just to let me say
I want to end it
I want to end it all
I wait but no one shows

I wait for them to find me
When all is said and done
but no one sees me
or hears the gun
the loud explosion
or the blood splatter
I wait for them to find me

I wait for them to cry
when they find my body
but no one sheds a tear
and they don't seem sorry
that I'm gone
and my life is over
I wait for them to cry

The weeks go by
but nothing occurs
Not even a proper funeral
led by a hearse
no one seems to notice
no one seems to care
The weeks go by

A single unmarked grave
with someone stood above
then they fade away
left not a trace in the mud
gone forever
and gone unnoticed
a single unmarked grave

This shouldn't happen
so please don't be distant
because this shouldn't exist
it should've ended different

This is Phil Pearce… In his own words… I wrote and performed the first time in November 2016 and fell in love with spoken word! I usually write around emotive topics such as addiction and knife crime.

This is a great poem about growing as a man, self-awareness and redemption. It shows how a man can make a change and how the power of words can have profound benefits.

Then and now:

The old crowd I used to be part of laugh when they hear I do poetry.
I've gone from being one of them,
to a stranger but that's ok with me

Cause it seems to me, they're all still living in those teenage ways,
Mad nights, no sleep, too much of whatever and not going home for days and
days.

I'm glad I can use my story, visit schools and stand in front of a class
And let all those impressionable teens know, that that life is a thing of the
past.

Because yeah, I've been to prison,
And yeah, I've done ridiculous amounts of drugs,
And yeah, I used to do bench press, never missed leg day and always finished
with shrugs!

But that was all for appearance
Everything, at that time was fake
And now that I've got my shit together
There's too much to lose now, there's too much at stake.

I've been watching videos on YouTube
Don't flop battles, poet's vs MC's
And it's as if they all have this same opinion,
That all poets like flowers and trees!

They think we all love herbal tea,
Eat vegan and dress the same way,
Now if I ever bump into one of these MC's
I'll have something to say!

Cause all they go on about is guns and being hard
And they all do talk the talk
But the difference between this poet and MC's
Is that I've walked that walk!

See, things have changed since I was young,
We now live in a 'copy and paste' generation,
Where we don't express ourselves with words anymore,
we choose emoji's with animation.

Life for me today is completely different,
It's less hectic and that's just how I want it,
The opportunity to sit and write these poems all day
Or even just peacefully sit.

Poetry has opened my eyes to the world
I see things in a different light,
It's almost as if I've been reborn again
or all of a sudden been given sight.

I've never bothered with parliament,
I don't understand all these political views,
And this might come across as ignorant
but I've never really paid much attention to the news!

I've never really thought outside of Leeds,
But one thing I am aware,
Is that nobody cares how much you know,
Until they know how much you care.

I've started reading up,
on problems that are relevant today
Like kids with different aspirations
all being taught the exact same way.

I know it's unrealistic to say,
that every student should have their own tutor,
But remember, Kids may only be a fraction of our population
but they are the whole fraction of our future.

We don't teach our kids the life skills,
That they'll one day need to know,
like how to budget, how to love,
how to cook food or make it grow.

Children's dreams and talents are getting missed,
And some home lives lead straight to criminality
To those kids my advice would be
Don't let your circumstances define your reality.

Let's use this gift of poetry for good,
Open a child's potential like an automatic door
And instead of watching their hearts grow sore
We can make their hearts grow and soar

Make them hang on to every word
and fall in love with the things you say,
And who knows, you might inspire that child,
to write a poem about their life one day!

This piece is a heartfelt poem about a mother's concern for her son. It shows how the mother feels helpless to her boy's suffering.

The writer has asked to remain anonymous but in her own words -

'This is about my youngest boy's battle with Social Anxiety Disorder and Depression.'

Happy Boy Gone...

Where has the happy boy gone?

The smiles of my childhood have faded like chalk dust on a weathered wall

Laugh lines replaced by furtive glances right and left...

Are people looking at me? Talking? Pointing? Laughing?

Where has the happy boy gone?

Pale skin. Grey eyes. Skeletal frame walking with hunched shoulders

Short, quick steps. Staring at the floor...can I get to the door?

No friends. No self-esteem. Feeling worthless as time passes me by.

Where has the happy boy gone?

Empty eyes staring down at picked skin. Hands shaking. Tears brimming.

I don't want to be alone. I want to be liked. Loved. Normal.

He is in there somewhere. Please help me find the happy boy gone...

This is Rosemary McLeish, in her own words:

I was born in Glasgow in 1945 and spent my school years in West Yorkshire. On leaving school I moved to London where I lived for twenty-one years, followed by 25 years in Glasgow where my husband worked at the university. I suffered from M.E. and various other illnesses for 17 years during which time I became a self-taught artist. I have suffered from depression for my whole life as well as having family with serious mental health issues. I started writing poetry when I was around 40 and in 2004-5 I did an MPhil in Creative Writing at Glasgow University. I have had poems published in anthologies, including several by Grey Hen Press, and magazines, as well as self-publishing two pamphlets and displaying poems in many exhibitions with my artworks. I am currently writing a book of memoir based on an exhibition I held in 2015 entitled "Not Doing the Ironing". The main piece was subsequently in an exhibition which toured the country for eighteen months. Since my husband retired in 2011 we have been living in East Kent, and I enjoy taking part in the local poetry reading circuit. I am this year on a Writers' Development Scheme based in Medway which is encouraging me to work towards a first collection.

This is a heart-breaking piece about the coming death of a much-loved brother.

My Brother's Face

My brother's face is grey today.

His breath comes in short gasps,

a heave like a hiccup in his chest,

inflating the worn-out hoover bag

of his tired lungs. His shoulders

hunch, then sag, hunch, then sag.

His eyes from under hooded lids

shoot a glance across the food at me,

then as quick away.

My brother's hair is grey today.

He's stopped dyeing it, chopped it off

around his ears without a mirror.

His skin's a sunk old sack.

Its deep folds gouge worn tracks

down his cheeks. He hasn't put his teeth in;

the image of his blood father, years ago,

escaped across the moor from Menston,

appearing, desperate, in our kitchen.

My brother's eyes are grey, today

as every day. They don't change.

He sits here eating dinner, which,

as on every Sunday, will travel

straight through him. He'll go

outside to smoke his fag, then

make Mum's cup of coffee, start

revving up for his ride home

to halfway house and curfew.

My brother's face is ravaged

with suffering unimaginable to me.

Each rough ragged breath

takes me back through fifty years

to the babe who cried and cried,

who barely slept, calmed only

by our hoarse-voiced lullabies.

That quick glance, though, is from

the old defeated man he has become.

My brother's eyes are grey today,

as grey as the day last year

he doused himself in gasoline

and held his lighter in his hand

weighing up which way to go.

His eyes, his laboured breath,

his dirty shirt and silence,

suggest another day of reckoning

won't be long. We don't speak.

This is Tony Noon, He lives in Mexborough, South Yorkshire. His poems have appeared widely in anthologies, local and national newspapers ... and on South Yorkshire buses.

Collections include Sporting Deviations and Evolution of Dragons from Blue Rose Press and Encore from Carrel Press.

More of Tony's work can be found online on Scriggler, The Blue Hour, and The Camel Saloon.

EMPTY FLOOR

The thin smile of acoustic air

anchors me;

ties me to the cold north

and it's histories of loss.

The echo of discarnate voice

draws me;

leads me to the dark valley

and it's legacies of ash.

The ricochet of regret

surrounds me;

backs me to the corner

and it's memories.

And lights are changing on an empty floor.

The lights are changing on an empty floor.

This is Rona Fitzgerald;

Rona Fitzgerald has poems in UK, Scottish, Irish magazines and anthologies both print and online. Most recent are in Poems for Grenfell Tower, Onslaught Press 2018, and #Me Too, Fair Acre Press, 2018.

In Rona's poem, the black dog again re-appears in this beautiful metaphorical piece.

Beyond Blue

I
Black dog's too tame
                    mines a wolf.

Hungry, ravishing
                    ready to pounce.

Words   music   joy
cannot penetrate my cave.

One foot in front of the other
                        food is fuel
wine, bitter herbs
                no lift, sense of abandon.

Love dims   Arctic night
                        sepulchre grey.

Energy dissipates
        start again tomorrow.

At night, demons come
regret   hurt   images

Your mine
says the beast, I will eat you!

No rest.

II

How do you feel?

My doctor asked, unclear
about my suffering.

Can you tell me more?

Nothing,
I feel nothing
        stasis   numb.

A deer shot in mid leap
          a seal swallowed by sharks.

The wordless wail of a woman
        whose baby is born still.

This is a poem by Leeds lad Mark Wilson. Mark is a dad of two and was a private hire driver. At the young age of forty Mark was diagnosed with Parkinson's disease.

This brutally honest piece is about how this affected him and how it showed him, perhaps, the true meaning of love.

Parkinson's

The time had come and I'd had enough

I felt so down things had become very tough

I felt on my own nobody cared

I felt so useless and very scared

Nobody loved me or had a thought for me

This was the only way out I could see

I climbed upstairs and sat on my bed

Dark thoughts were running round my head

I poured the drink and put tablets in my hand

When they found me I'm sure they'd understand

Just why I had to do it why I had to get out

They'd be better off without me I had no doubt

I sat back and was ready to end it all

My phone then rang so I answered the call

It was my daughter to ask if I was ok

I couldn't tell her what I was doing that day

It was then I had a change of mind

How could I leave them my loved ones behind?

I was being selfish to all my family and friends

It's them that would be suffering in the end

People did love me now I was sure

Even if I didn't realise all this before

This is a short anonymous poem about the loss of identity and how it makes this person feel.

No One

My name is No-one

I am somebody's daughter, somebody's mother, somebody's sister

But still, I have no name

I am faceless

Just the person who is here

This is a poem by Rhianna France.

Rhianna is a 17-year-old student from Leeds and has already won several competitions for her work.

She wrote this mature piece of poetry, reflecting the anxiety and pain felt by a teenage girl, when she was only 15…

Freak

Freak

Monster

The names they call me

The devil on my shoulder

The voices in my mind

Worthless

Pathetic

The list goes on and on

And whilst my heart is saying 'Do one thing'

My mind is reeling saying 'Don't listen to it'

My heart is saying to love

My mind is saying I can't, I never can, I never was and I never will be

But whilst you're there eating what you want I'm starving myself

Afraid of what you might think if I tell the truth

Afraid you will judge me for battling with things you can't see

Things you can't show

Things you don't even know are there until everything comes crashing down

But I'm afraid

I'm afraid I'll lose this fight

I'm afraid that I'll be loved, but not love back

I'm afraid to be hurt because the scars and burns I bare, are too much live through again

Too much for a teenager who has nothing to worry about

Too much for a child with a perfect life

Too much for someone who is constantly living in fear of themselves and their mind

I go through this daily.

So, you can sit there, enjoying that low mark you got on that test

Whilst I worry if I can make someone proud when I gotten marks higher

You can sit and enjoy your meals

Whilst I worry about putting on another pound

I drown myself in my fears and worries, and as a border

I use oversized clothes to keep everything in

To stop this thing from leaking everywhere bringing not only me, but everyone else down

And sometimes the blackness is comforting

The thoughts of blood and cuts are so known to me, that I find myself absorbed in a pain that isn't there

In an emotion I cannot feel

So, enjoy your time, because I might not be here for long.

This is Tony Noon again with a beautiful metaphorical poem.

BROKEN THINGS

You knew these streets like a satnav,

saw them Sunday best and wore their tee shirts.

Now rubble footprints kick half moved earth

and gangs of buddleia gather to heckle.

Only you are waved through.

In this no frills town you were a Godsend.

Broke bread with the vanished

and drank with them from jam jars.

Week after week beneath the smog

you were a lifeline, testing vital signs.

Mending broken things.

This is E.C. Price -

E. C. Price is a writer based in West Yorkshire. She was born and brought up in the shadow of the Bronte sisters and now lives with her wife and four-legged fur baby in the heart of the rhubarb triangle. She is currently working on her first novel.

Here is a lovely short story showing the impact of depression on motivation and how that can spin into anxiety.

The Bicycle Was in Its Usual Place

"The bicycle was in its usual place…"

…. But the rider wasn't. Not today. Today she couldn't face leaving the house, or her room – sod it, the whole hog – today she couldn't face leaving her bed. Some invisible, yet powerful force pressed her deeper into the mattress, preventing her body from moving. She could just about move her eyes. Blink, blink. The world was closing in on her, compressing her into a tiny ball. If she moved, something bad would happen. Someone would see her, someone would know she was there, and that was too much to cope with today.

She had been due to start work over an hour ago, but a quick text message to the boss put paid to that. The frequency of her sick days was probably becoming an issue, but that could be dealt with some other time. Not today. There was nothing special about today, it just wasn't the *right* day. Unwanted thoughts had found their way into her head overnight - the "what ifs?" and the self-doubt she fought against daily had caught her unaware in a moment of weakness – when she was asleep! They're cunning like that. So cunning that she'd fallen asleep feeling okay about herself, her life and her world – but then woken up like this, feeling as though everything was crashing down around her.

She lay there for hours, silent except for the occasional rustle of sheets, and listened to life going on outside. Dogs barked, kids on the trampoline 2 doors down alternately shrieked with joy and argued with each other, car doors were slammed, and engines roared. As neighbours went about their business they issued their obligatory cursory greetings and grunts belying long-running grudges or engaged in small talk and gossip. She couldn't make out all the words, but the intonation implied that it was scandalous. It was probably far from it, just made up drama and she wanted no part of it. The everyday lies, the deceit, the mundane stuff, and the people! People were just so tiresome, interaction so exhausting...

Suddenly, three loud bangs on the door jolted her from her eavesdropping. Her skin prickled, her eyes widened, and she could feel her heart thudding against her ribs as if it was trying to burst out.

What the hell was that? Why is someone banging on my door? What do they want? They must know I'm here! I've been found out!

She threw the bedsheets over her head and stayed as small and still as she could.

Please go away, please go away, just leave me alone, I promise I'll go to work tomorrow. I just need a break today. Just for today. Please leave me alone!

Nausea gripped her. Breathing was no longer an automatic reflex but took a mighty effort for little return - shallow and frantic, though she tried her hardest to extend each breath it was just another failure. Drawing her legs up to her chest she clung tightly to her knees and started to weep. Tears of sadness, tears of fear, but mostly tears of confusion. After a while her muscles started to ache, so she gently released the grip on her knees and stretched her legs out, slowly and carefully to minimise the noise. Someone may be listening. She held her stretched out pose for a few more minutes, listening intently for any sounds – but there were none.

From nowhere, she felt the over-riding urge to get out of bed. She knew though, that if she got up, she should really have gone into work today. Obviously, she should have gone in anyway – there was nothing physically wrong with her, but if she stayed in bed she could convince herself she was poorly. As the guilt crept in, she veered into her familiar self-destruct mode. She knew exactly where her brain was taking her, but she felt powerless to change its course.

What was I thinking of? All those people I've let down at work and if mum finds out I've done it again she'll be so mad at me – I'm such a waste of space. A pathetic, worthless, waste of space.

The pattern was always the same. The journey begins in self-pityland, followed by a quick jaunt to fear and scaredville. Lunch would be taken at the self-loathing brasserie with a brief visit to anger central to round things off for the day. She could then justify her desperate attempt at an early night in bed which she knew would consist of a substantial amount of desperation and sleeplessness.

Shaking her head in exasperation at herself, she swung her legs out of bed and padded barefoot into the bathroom. She grasped the basin with both hands and stared at her watery-eyed reflection in the dirty mirror above.

What an absolute joke you are. What are you doing with your life? You really need to sort yourself out because before too long you'll lose everybody and everything you have, and then you will have something to be bloody miserable about!

She needed to shower. Quickly. Otherwise returning to bed would become a more tempting proposition. She turned on the taps and stepped over the side of the bath in to the cold stream, but rather than shrinking back out she shuddered and waited in place. Gradually the temperature increased, and its warmth clung to her body like a comforting arm around her shoulders. She knew she didn't deserve such a feeling though and crumpling into a heap, she began to cry again.

There must be more to life than this pitiful existence. Surely, I'm not asking too much or maybe I am? I don't know. But I just need to get out of this rut and this cycle I'm perpetually living in. I just wish someone would help me! I just need help.

She clambered to her feet and held her face close to the shower head to soothe her face and eyes.

What was it all those books had said? 'If you want to make something happen **you** *need to make change. You're the only one that can make something happen'. Well that's fine if you haven't got a head full of negativity and doubt! Stupid books anyway – they know nothing about me.*

Squeezing shampoo into her hand, she roughly scrubbed at her hair and scalp.

Okay, fine! She shouted at her head. She even stamped her foot, and then immediately rolled her eyes at her own tantrum. *Okay, come on, what can I change, what do I want?*

She took the rest of her shower to question her own mind and think hard about what it was she did want. What would make her happy? After she was dried off, dressed and downstairs with a coffee held tightly in her hands, she knew. She just simply wanted to not be herself anymore.

Haha! Simply! Good one.

Shut up head!

Maybe I could try and recreate myself? What if I just created a whole new identity? Just became someone else? I could sack off work, move somewhere else, get a whole new group of friends – move on and recreate! That was it, the grand plan, it could work!

Building a nest of cushions on the sofa and drawing the blanket over herself, she gave herself permission to explore this plan in more detail. She longed for the arrival of the next day now, when she could grab her bicycle from its usual place and ride off on an adventure. She craved the feeling of the wind in her hair, a glow in her cheeks, an intense burn in her legs and the utter exhilaration of freedom. Freedom from the shackles of work, free from her house, but most of all from her own mind. She would be able to do anything she wanted, and anything was possible. She might cycle for miles and stop to have a picnic at the side of a meandering stream, basking in the glorious sunshine. She might keep going, cycle off into the sunset, stumble upon a ruined cottage, buy it from the owner, do it up and live happily ever after. Tomorrow could bring so much. She just had to get through the rest of today to reach it. That was it, the plan was firm in her mind. Today was for planning, making lists, researching routes and stop off points, exploring new areas online ready to set out confidently in person. The wheels were well and truly in motion – well, they were being oiled at least.

She stayed up long into the night, lost in a world of thinking and planning for tomorrow. The occasional slip of guilt crept into her head that this energy could have been used at work, but she batted it away. She had spent a lot of her time trying to please others and trying to make others happy. So much of her emotional energy had gone into making sure others were content that she'd lost any idea of how to keep herself fulfilled. She had no idea who she was anymore and had no idea how the happy go lucky child she'd been had got into her current mess. She felt like life had landed her with a huge debt, when she didn't even know she was in arrears...

"The bicycle was in its usual place…"

…But the rider wasn't. Not yet, however. She had used all the mental energy she could muster to drag herself out of bed, and she was making her way out of the house. She would be late for work, but she didn't really care. Her plans had crashed and burned in bed overnight when her unwanted thoughts had paid another night-time visit, but this time to steal her hopes and dreams.

As she stepped out into her yard and turned to lock the door, she brushed a tear away from her eye with her forefinger.

'Morning! Lovely day? How are you doing?'

Startled by the voice, she glanced over her shoulder where her neighbour was pegging washing on the line. The sky was a dazzling blue and the sun was just peeping over the rooftops out back. It probably was a lovely day, if you were into that sort of thing. But she wasn't. Not today.

'Oh, you know' she replied, 'not bad thanks, and you?' She turned away as she rolled her eyes at herself.

'Not too bad myself thanks, have a good day luvvie!' and with that, her neighbour turned on her heels and went back indoors humming a vague tune.

Expelling a deep breath, she took the handles of the bicycle and wheeled it to the side of the road. She sat astride and pushed off. By the time she'd reached the bottom of the short hill however, her tears were flowing, and she had to stop and get off for fear of crashing. She dragged her bicycle out of the road, propped it against a wall and sat on a nearby bench. Cradling her head in her hands, tears seeped out between her fingers and ran down her arms.

'Whatever he's done love it's not worth it – nobody should make you feel like this. Get rid of him. That's what I'd do!' A little grey-haired lady with a couple of shopping bags had joined her on the bench.

Inside, she screamed *There is no man, it's me! It's my own head making me feel like this!* Thankfully, her mouth didn't betray her. 'It's just such a mess, I'm such a mess,' she stuttered from behind her tear-soaked hands.

'You're alright love, nothing a tissue and a dab of make-up won't sort out'

'No, you don't understand. *I'm* just such a mess!'

'It'll all come out in the wash. Now, if I were you, I'd get myself back off home and have what you young 'uns call a "duvet day" and it'll all be right as rain – you'll see!' The old lady stood up and flagged down the approaching bus. Climbing aboard she turned at looked at the forlorn figure still sitting on the bench, 'go on, get yourself home' she urged.

I don't suppose one more day could harm could it? After all, it may make an illness seem more believable if I have 2 days off.

With little more encouragement needed she plodded back up the hill towards home, leaning on the handlebars. Her eyes were fixated on the wheels as they turned. Even this simple metal contraption was taunting her now, as she thought back to the previous day's worries about being stuck in a cycle of despair.

The old lady seemed wise, another duvet day will give me time to sort my head out and think about what I'm going to do with myself. Tomorrow is another day, and who knows what it might bring?

Anne Rhodes with another well written poem covering the subject of freedom.

Freedom

Freedom as a word has depth and meaning

And yet be so difficult to maintain.

One day the spirit can be uplifted

The cry of Freedom is so strong and true.

Freedom from fear can mean separation

Leaving behind the causes of heartache

Starting afresh, though it takes some courage,

Can be a freedom for which you have dreamed.

Freedom from the pain brought on by beatings

Freedom to live as you yourself want to.

Freedom from the pain of those cruel blows

Freedom to be your own person at last.

Freedom from pain of a different nature

Bodily pain which you wish was long gone.

Pain of an illness, or old aching bones.

Medication brings freedom for a while.

On bad days the only thing to cling to

Is that maybe, just maybe, tomorrow

Will bring sunlight and freedom just for yourself

Freedom to relish and be thankful for.

This is Catherine Whittaker again with a truth that many with depression face, the deep dark nights.

I won't be Returning

I'm off the pills you'll be pleased to know
feeling great in the clear-eyed morning,
but the nights still fall hard and slow.

It's great to see buds unwrap start to grow
it's even good to feel my old tangled yearning,
I'm off the pills you'll be pleased to know.

Sometimes I swing too fast from high to low
I'm strong enough to ignore the warning,
but the nights still fall hard and slow.

Afternoons often funnel into shadow
but it's all right, I'm still awake, still burning.
I'm off the pills you'll be pleased to know.

It's fine to hear your voice again, although
at times it fades, it's ok, I'm still learning,
but the nights still fall hard and slow.

I'm brave enough, not too scared to throw
out the shadows calling; I won't be returning.
I'm off the pills you'll be pleased to know
but the nights still fall so hard and slow.

This is Krissie Dee Murray, in her own words... I'm 17 and from Leeds. I have been writing poems for a few years and do it to have an outlet for my emotions without feeling like I'm burdening other people with them. I love being creative and in my spare time I write poems, song lyrics, plays and story ideas. I come from a single parent family with my mum and two older brothers. I'm in college at the moment studying psychology, sociology and music technology. When I'm older I want to become a counsellor to help people. I consider myself as a very sociable person and love meeting new people that I could be friends with. Family is very important to me as I love spending time with my aunts, uncles and cousins who I sometimes help look after.

Here is a heartfelt piece written with maturity and feeling.

Ragdoll

Laid on the floor
are my lifeless limbs
then up to the sky like I have wings
thrown around
from place to place
all I am
is a waste of space
Just a ragdoll
to be flung around
I can't do anything
can't even make a sound
broken and stitched together
so now I have scars
all I want to do is reach for the stars
Time is ticking
it's running out
and deep within
I start to doubt
I can't do this
I'll just fail
suddenly, it slows
I feel so frail
I'm trying to save
my broken heart
but limb from limb
I'm ripped apart
crying out
begging you please
kill me now
and put me at ease

This is Miranda Wright, in her own words…Miranda is an ex-teacher, who has lived in Beeston for the past 30 years. In the past, she has written play scripts for school performances, and had a couple of poems published in anthologies many years ago. She sometimes writes personalised poems for friends or colleagues, but she has more recently started writing stories for children. She is married, with two grown up children, and she likes dancing, cats, gardening, bird-watching and going for long walks, especially on the beach. She has an awareness of mental health issues both from first- and second-hand experience.

This is a great poem about the mask's women wear.

War Paint

In your ivory tower, you sit, surrounded by your pots and jars,

Your powders and your paints.

A modern day Rapunzel, or a lady of Shalott,

You gaze at your mirror, behind the voile.

You tint, you highlight, you conceal,

Creating a daily work of modern art,

Before you show yourself to the world outside,

Exhausted people on a bus, a tired taxi driver, people on a train,

All with their heads down, studying their social media,

The unreal reality of today.

Once, when you were very small,

We watched a lady on TV, with her dog

And they called on us to come outside,

To see the nature and the adventure of the world.

To explore a forest, and to watch a bird,

Or pick up shells upon a beach.

Happy childhood spontaneity!

 Get up, get showered, get dressed and go

(Don't worry about face or hair – you are a beauty)

I wish, more than anything, that you could do that now.

Penny Blackburn

Originally from Mirfield in West Yorkshire, Penny Blackburn now lives in the North East of England and is a teacher by profession. As well as writing poetry she enjoys performing it 'off-page' as part of local open mic and spoken word events. She also writes short fiction and was the winner of the 2017 Story Tyne competition as well as being runner up in the Readers' Digest 100-word-story competition 2018

Here is fantastic piece. Depression erodes self-confidence and this poem expresses that vividly.

Chemical Change

Internal flow of snow-ice melt
Clear-cold, harsh-stream
Adrenaline torrent.

The density of bones – retracted,
Felt deep in limbs and under skin.

Complacency beaten by hollow knowledge
Certainty leaked out of porous gaps
Confidence transformed from 'always' into 'never'
Self –belief vaporised from solid into gas.

This is Michelle Graham, in her own words:

I've had a lot of emotional, physical and sexual abuse as a kid and adult. I left home at 15 and lived on streets, started drinking at 15, lost a partner due to heroin at 19. Never really recovered, have mental health issues and now diagnosed with bi polar, and hear voices. Moved to Yorkshire 4 years ago after having a break down, since moving here I learnt to channel my emotions and feelings into writing it in poetry form and painting abstract art, I've been sober for 11 months now and in therapy, I did a detox programme with turning point which basically saved my life. I like to share my poetry with others that maybe going through same thing

This is an honest poem about the scars we have. Those given, those physical and those within our own mental health.

Scars

Wish poetry was my only self-harm, I could write out my lows, instead of blood see words, instead of a blade I have a keyboard.

I wish I could write about dancing in the seas amongst the whispering waves, harm isn't just cutting isn't just you hate yourself.

Fiery red

Anger

Builds up inside

Got to get them out.

Turning the blade into my keyboard, the only one to be trusted, the one I turn to when it's too much.

Turn harm into words, words into sentences, getting the pain out without the scars.

Blood rushing out causing more pain than the relief of letting the pain out, scars, pain, turning it to words led by the pen.

Robin Nixon is a singer / songwriter / poet, and the author of over 500 magazine articles and more than 30 books on subjects ranging from computing to motivational psychology and science fiction. Robin is a regular on the music and poetry circuits throughout the south east.

This is a beautifully written heartfelt piece, about the loss of love and how we try to hide the hurt we always feel.

You're No-Longer There

When you see me quietly sleeping

You think that I am peacefully dreaming

But my heart is secretly weeping

And my lungs are silently screaming

I see you every day; I watch you in your chair

I hear the words you say, but you're no-longer there

When you hear me placidly breathing

Or think that I am passively speaking

In my head I'm acidly seething

And my stomach is violently heaving

So bright but now so dead; the love I used to know

How can you share my bed, when you left so long ago?

When you find me socially mixing

My laughter is fully convincing

But all reason is totally missing

And rhyme entirely constricting

I see you every day; I watch you in your chair

I hear the words you say, but you're no-longer there

So bright but now so dead; the love I used to know

How can you share my bed, when you left so long ago?

This is Elisabeth Straw again with a sad tale of how the smallest of thing can break the camel's back.

The Rolls We Play

It all started with a sausage roll. A simple and quite humble sausage roll. To think that something so unassuming could lead to the cataclysm that it did, is incredible. But I suppose it says more about my relationship with him than anything else. A sausage roll could cause a monumental humdinger of an argument and lead to the break-up of a marriage. Who was I trying to kid? That sausage roll was innocent.

I had booked a week away in Brixham in Devon. The house looked perfect to me. Within a short walking distance of the sea and right near the town centre. Brixham looked incredibly pretty and had a plethora of seafood restaurants and plenty of culture. I envisaged lovely, long walks by the harbour and sitting in a café drinking rosé as we watched the sun go down. Trips to galleries and local museums. Making sandcastles and collecting shells. The children would love it with its replica of the Golden Hind too, lots of pirates and swash buckling! Ahoy there me hearties!

The journey down was horrific. It must have taken us over eight hours to get there and most of it stuck in traffic jams. The trouble with such a journey is that it can make or break a holiday. Trapped in a car going nowhere with two whining kids, doesn't present the ideal start to a holiday, let alone the marriage that is virtually crumbling. A few weeks prior to this we had separated for the umpteenth time.

It didn't look like the holiday was going to happen. Yet again he'd walked out on me for some ridiculous reason. His brother had told him that I'd been trying to match make or something similar and he believed him. This had caused a disagreement which rose to an argument which developed into a physical battle and culminated in him storming out. The fact is though, that if someone keeps walking out on you every time you have a quarrel, then eventually you learn to cope on your own and live without him. You might think this was his way of avoiding conflict. It wasn't. It was a control mechanism. He'd ring me several days later when I was at my wits' end trying to deal with a baby and a child with special needs and then issue his demands. His favourite phrase, 'Do this or else!' I'd end up giving in and agreeing to anything just so that I could have some help with the kids.

By the time we arrived in Brixham and found the accommodation, we were all famished and desperate to escape each other. Sometime apart at this point would have been ideal. Sadly, that is not always possible on a family holiday. Instead we walked down to the harbour and sat outside to eat some fish and chips. The squawking caws of the seagulls draped a wave of relief over us which seemed to sweep our stress away. Finally, I was starting to relax and there was a certain optimism in me that this could possibly turn out to be a decent holiday. We held hands as we walked home. I knew I loved him, but I could never accept the fact that I didn't really like him. It was the perfect example of not being able to reconcile my heart and my head.

I don't know what it is about holidays, but I am always eager to make a cooked breakfast every morning. I do it even now. I start the holiday saying there is no way that I will cook and then before you know it I am doing hash browns, egg, bacon, sausage and fried bread to feed the five thousand, not to mention the mushrooms and black pudding. So, full of exuberance, I rose early and cooked breakfast. We all had a good share and decided to find somewhere interesting where we could walk off our breakfast. It was quite a dull, drizzling morning and so we thought a trip to the local Brixham Heritage Museum might be a good idea.

They had a huge toy display and I knew my son, with his love of teddies, cars and lorries and trains would absolutely love it. So, we went off and entered the crammed museum with its several floors of all kinds of Brixham artefacts. As we were about to view the first exhibits he turned to me and said in front of the curator,

'God this is bloody awful. I'll see you in the café.'

'Great' I thought, 'Leave me to look after the kids. As usual.' He raced upstairs. I never knew why he always had to do that. Say something inappropriate in front of someone and ruin their day. I just saw that as downright nasty. He could never empathise or understand how other people felt. It was all about him and his needs.

Contrary to what his thoughts were, we delighted in the exhibits. It was jam packed with all kinds of relics and the staff could not do enough for us. Their enthusiasm was infectious, and we spent a good hour looking at everything as well as pressing buttons, watching slide shows and dressing up. The children were desperate to buy some souvenirs and so we went to the café.

He was sitting in the café. He glared at me as though I was a child who needed scolding.

'What took you so long? This place is utter shit.'

I tried to ignore him and made my way towards the cashier to buy a drink.

'I got you a drink ages ago. It's here. Drink it.'

I didn't want an argument. I just wanted to enjoy my holiday, so I relented and started to drink the tepid coffee. He pushed a plate towards me with a sausage roll on it.

'Here I got you this.'

'I'm fine. I'm still full up from breakfast.' I really had regretted that last hash brown. I felt bilious and nauseous.

'You're so bloody cantankerous, aren't you? You won't ever do anything to please anyone will you? You are such a fucking bitch.' The more he spoke the more the anger in him grew. He was getting louder with each word.

'You're so fucking unreasonable. You keep me waiting in here for this shit museum and now you won't eat this fucking sausage roll.' With that he picked up the plate and threw it at me. I was getting quite used to this. He stormed out of the building as I stood there aghast. The children were still absorbed in looking at the souvenirs.

'Can I have this one Mummy?' William held up a giant pencil.

'Yes of course.' I stumbled. I looked at the cashier and felt the embarrassment intensifying inside me.

'I'm so sorry. I think he's just having a bad day!' I don't know why I even tried to excuse him. There was no civilised excuse for that.

The children and I made our way back downstairs and out of the front door. We saw him almost fly past with his engine roaring from the acceleration. That was it. He'd gone. He'd left us in Devon. Over two hundred miles away from home. A wife and two children stranded. And all because of a sausage roll.

I went back to the house and did what I always did when I wanted to cry. I drank a bottle of wine and waited for the tears to flow and engulf me so that I could sense the physical pain of my loss. Yet I didn't feel guilty. I felt let down. My upset began to turn into anger. How dare he do that to me and the kids? What an evil, morally bankrupt bastard! I really wanted to hold onto the anger, but I wasn't strong enough to hold back the tears as I gradually realised, 'How on earth am I going to get home?' I knew I wasn't going to get any sleep that night.

A great nonsense poem from David Bradshaw escribing the foibles of a 'Prancing Poet'

Pimpernel the Prancing Poet

Pimpernel the prancing poet,

Is the most bizarre of folk,

Because he wears exploding hats,

He pens his odes through clouds of smoke.

Pimpernel the prancing poet,

Skips around his garden shed,

Busy writing rhyming couplets,

While juggling with loaves of bread.

Pimpernel the prancing poet,

Capers freely through the trees,

Composing limericks and haikus,

Wearing cymbals on his knees.

Pimpernel the prancing poet,

Pirouettes about the place,

Jotting down his joyful verse,

With toast and jam upon his face.

Pimpernel the prancing poet,

Dances jigs in the pouring rain,

While he scribbles down his sonnets,

For Pimpernel is quite insane.

Another by Frank Varley. This is a great funny poem about those devices that now seem to be smarter than us!

Ok Google

That thing that I say "ok Google" to

I've forgotten what you're called

But to you, if I don't say please and thank you

My wife she is appalled.

That thing that I say "ok Google "to

Has got to be shown respect

You're only the size of a large mince pie

Still I feel I have to genuflect

My wife says "that's a lady giving you those answers

Who knows what feelings she may have?

You've got to treat her kindly

Just like the lady in my Sat Nav ".

Your assistance when we're baking

Produces results very seldom seen

You can time me 20 minutes

And not fall asleep at 19

You're the one with all the answers

You can play me any song

If I ask you what the score is

You never get it wrong

So, whether it's "ok Google play radio 2"

Or "ok Google what's the time?"

You'll always get a please and thank you

From these lips of mine.

This is Mark Wilson again with a poem about depression and hope.

Depression

When depression grabs hold it's so hard to shake

It plays with your mind and keeps you awake

It puts thoughts inside your head

Thoughts that you really do dread

You're not worth much it best if you just go

What do you do you just don't know

Will they be better off without you?

The doubts are hard to go through

Is suicide the only way out?

That's the thing you think about

Although you might feel you're all alone

You are not on your own

So if you feel it's the only way

Just take a step back you only have to say

That you don't want your life to end

Talk to someone they will be your friend

Together you will find you're very strong

And those dark thoughts you had were so wrong

Another poem by Anne Rhodes. This one is about out observations of the refugees and dispossessed.

IF IN EXCESS OF PAIN OR GRIEF THEY STAMMER "WHY?"

I sweat in fear, my heart still hammers loud

I've lost all I own beyond this sack held near

They burned us out, we fled completely cowed.

In darkness, children's voices cried in fear.

Many are too old for such long travelling

Some left behind us as we staggered on

We worried at our energy unravelling

But now through crowds, the camps we gaze upon.

Plastic shelters as far as the eye can see

At least the soldiers are left far behind.

Thousands gather, all as weary as me.

How can they help us all – though folk look kind.

We are poor and scorned, without roof or bread.

Everyone needs compassion. Don't you? Don't I?

Nothing's like it used to be, some folk said

Why does mankind hate fellow man, oh why?

Give me a job and I will do my best

I'm a refugee, through no fault of mine.

Each one of us will make the same request

An answered prayer from you will be a sign.

This is Kevin Chorlton, in his own honest words.

Born into a background just above poverty, no car, 3 boys one bedroom. Dad always trying to kill himself always got me. he died of cancer in 79 I was just 22. my own depression was always around even though I was good at hiding it. I was a top youth player at footy and was with a lot of clubs Everton, Middlesbrough, Luton etc... but I never stayed long because I always worried about my Mam. My depression was, and still is, controlled by tablets but I have a good lifestyle.

Kevin is an ex pat who now lives in the sunny climes of Cyprus.

Galaxy

Open your eyes and what do you see, a sky full of stars and eternity.

Close your eyes and the world goes dark, reality bites and the world is stark.

No trust no loyalty, and no love, this reality when you move your eyes from above.

The world is small and a sullen place, nothing like wonderful outer space.

I wish the stars could be my home, billions of miles but never alone.

Brian Mack

Taking a break from his day job as Technical Business Development Manager. Brian Mack expresses his creativity by writing and exercising his mind away from the factual to fiction, creative writing or comments in his favourite genre sarcasm.

This is a great piece by Brian he cleverly plays with the word 'mind' to reinforce the poems impact.

Phrase your mind.

What's your **State of mind** they always ask? You're just playing **Mind games** expecting an answer.

Do you really care about **what's on my mind**, what I really think? My thoughts are mine; my conscious state belongs to me and me alone. Please get out of my head, **get out of my mind**, my life is my own for me to own and me alone.

But all you say in return is, **never mind**, please **frame your mind**, you're **caught in two minds**, **mind how you go**, and if you're not careful you'll **lose your mind**.

But I have a **mind of my own**, I have an **open mind**. This should not be a battle of **hearts and minds;** I **know my own mind**. So, I can set *your* **mind at ease**, if you have a **mind's eye** and a **mindset** to do so. It's a question of **mind over matter**, yet you believe I'll **lose my mind**, thinking I've only **half a mind**. **Never mind**, I hear you say just go to the gym and exercise as they say *"a healthy body and healthy mind "*. Or "go on holiday because **travel broadens the mind"**.

Your comments had never **crossed my mind;** your words

don't **blow my mind**. You think your reasoning is **mind blowing** and **mind boggling**, expecting me to **change my mind**.

Don't underestimate me I'm of **sound mind**, so **mind your own business**, and **never you mind** about criticising me. **My mind is my own**, to do as I please. It's my soul, my inner self, my friend and my enemy. I **control my mind** *and* **my mind controls me** together we conquer all as **great minds think alike**. Don't ever **cross your mind**, as a **mind is a terrible thing to waste**.

You are what you are, indisputably you, unique and individual **in spirit and in mind**. You are one in a billion an original person that needs to remember you have *a **mind of your own*** love it and it will love you.

Stefan Grieve is a writer based in Wakefield, West Yorkshire. He is the chairperson of Wakefield Word, as well as being on the committee of the Black Horse Poets. Along with all the other writing groups he attends, Stefan can be found at a sizeable amount of spoken word events too. Sometimes he can be found at the occasional literature festival. He has recently been published on the website of 'Fairlight books' with the story: 'The café at night', as well as various publications locally.

Here is his sharply written short story...Black Dog

Black Dog

There was a howl. It was a howl dripping with sadness, regret, and hunger. It caused the air to creak and the darkness to become darker, and colder. That's how it felt for Patches, anyway, when he heard that call as he turned the corner street late that Autumn night. The howling got louder and louder and his breath got colder, solidifying into a mist. It was then he looked over his shoulder. A mass of black smoke hung in the air, with flashes of teeth, eyes, and claws.

He looked at the bottom of the bottle of booze he was holding, to see if it held a label warning: Careful, side effects may include psychotic visions. It did not. So, he ran. Then he heard the voice. But it wasn't a voice outside; it was within. It was his own voice.

There is no use.

I will catch you.

You cannot get away

Then I will eat you

And no one will cry

No one will care.

And as he tried to get away he felt his leg getting heavier, and himself getting more tired, more than he had ever been. It was if the whole world was holding him down. That was then he decided to give up, and he stopped and let the darkness take him…

"This looks nice," Said Opal, with her wide smile letting more of the light in as the dusty grey van bore through the dull countryside.

"Oh yeah, if you like you like your little towns to be in the middle of nowhere through miles of empty fields," Said Pete, light glinting on his round glasses as he drove the van

"You're never happy with anything, are you?"

Pete sighed, ruffling his black, wavy hair "It's just sometimes I just don't find anything to be happy about. I don't know how you do it, Oppy."

"Years of practice," She said with a smile, and then added, "Oh, stop here."

The van stopped with a shuddering lurch. They were by a shop on its own, old brick and rust.

Opal got out of the van, her wild mousy hair caught in the wind as she went into the shop.

For such a small looking shop on the outside, it was surprising that it was even smaller seeming on the inside. There was everything she'd expect to be in the shop, and more. She found it remarkably cosy.

She got what she needed (a drink, a toothbrush, and after much careful thought, a comb,) and she brought it to the counter, to the man who worked there.

He was pale, with a gaunt face and heaviness around blue eyes that didn't look like they had been blessed with much sleep.

Opal smiled at him and was rewarded with a smile back. It was a smile that was slow to form, but she found rewarding.

They didn't share a single word, but the smile seemed to be enough.

Opal left the shop shedding the anxiety she had about this trip to this town that she had hidden from her boyfriend, and a new sense of hope held heavy in her heart.

Yes, she thought, things would be alright.

"So, did the shop owner try to kill you?"

"What?" Opal asked wearily, only half-hearing through a yawn, then, "No, he just smiled at me,"

"Oh," Said Pete, "So he was probably just thinking of killing you."

Opal hit him on the shoulder.

"Ow!"

"You big baby," She smiled with no trace of malice, but a reliable playfulness.

The van lurched forward.

They soon arrived into the town, driving past small, yellowing buildings sometimes broke up by modern architecture, like supermarkets and some trendy cafés and restaurants.

The van shuddered to a halt.

Opal look out and saw there were parked near a darkened pub, with a sign swinging by it with its name, 'Baskerville'

"Why have we stopped here?"

"Because I need to eat to live, and to drink, to forgot that I'm here," He said and got out.

Opal followed him.

The pub was mostly in darkness, and Opal suspected that the moods of the inhabitants were mostly in darkness as well. Pete felt at home.

The pub goers hardly moved the faces from there pint glasses as they entered. A few offered a side-look and a frown. Opal felt her optimistic weapon of a smile would be overpowered here and may even attract scorn, so she kept it sheathed. For now, at least.

"Do you do food?" Pete asked the barman.

"We do beef."

"Beef?"

"Beef and chips."

"Well… that sounds lovely,"

Opal could tell he wasn't trying to be sarcastic. His sarcasm was…less subtle than most people's sarcasm.

The barman nodded.

"What would you like?" Pete asked him.

"I'm fine thanks, I'm not hungry."

"To drink?"

"Orange juice."

"Right, a pint of orange and a pint of erm… Booze. Probably of the beer variety, thanks, we will sit… there," Pete said gesturing to an empty table.

The barman nodded, Pete tried a smile. What he achieved was an awkward smirk.

They went to a table and sat down, putting their drinks down on the table in front of them

"Well, this is… nice," Said Pete.

"You're only saying that because you feel uncomfortable and intimidated, otherwise you would be your normal, miserable self."

"Alright, alright not so loud," Pete said, then added, "I thought you were all through the smiles and positiveness, anyway,"

"There is a time and a place, I guess," Opal said, "And a smile's not worth anything if it's insincere, in fact, it can be poisonous."

Pete frowned at her. Not because of what she said, but because of her heavy expression.

"Opal… Oppy, are you ok?"

"Yes… well no," She said, then looked away, and Pete could see something wet and shiny glint in her eye.

"It's just you know, sometimes it's hard to smile, with you know, mood."

"I know," Said Pete, and held her hand, caressing it, "You've been through so much recently but you're being so strong, this year has been hard for you, god knows, it would be hard for anyone."

"Thanks," Opal said, sniffing and mustering up a smile.

"No, I mean it. Now we will just deliver this package to whoever this 'Doctor Limbic' is and…"

"Oh, I'd be careful of him," Said a man nearby, holding a frothy beer.

"Why?" Asked Pete, expression darkening.

"I've heard things."

"Oh yeah? What kind of things?"

"Dark things,"

"Well, that narrows it down a bit then…"

"Pete!" Opal hissed, "Go on," she said.

"Well, I daren't say no more about that man, but I think you can't have come at a worse time to our village, they've been…"

"Murders," Said another man pitching in, nodding his head sagely.

"What!?" Pete spluttered.

"That there have," Said the first man, "well deaths at least, bodies found with their life, drained out of them. Or even supped. Like a man would sup on a pint."

"Oh lovely," Pete said.

"Just you be careful," they said back.

The barman put his plate down of beef and chips. It was indeed beef and chips, or at least bared a thin resemblance to something that was once alive, slumped next to something that may have been cut from a potato. Or some other vegetable. Maybe.

"Well if the beef doesn't kill me off I have been murdered like a pint of beer to look forward too,"

"Well, I see you've become more honest," Opal said curtly.

"Well you know," Pete said, taking a swig of his pint, "Booze helps with unlocking the finer virtues in such wayward souls."

"Is it just me, or has it got darker earlier today?" Pete asked.

"You're a permanent pessimist Pete, to you, it's always darker earlier," Opal said.

"Well, aren't you getting in?" Pete asked her, as adjusted himself in the driving seat.

"Well, on the way here I saw a café that looked quite nice and now I'm a bit hungry and…"

"Was it the café that had the old woman sitting outside with the little dog?"

"The adorable puppy, you mean?"

Pete smiled and shook his head, "I will come back to pick you up in half an hour, do you want a lift?"

"Nah, it's fine love, I'll walk,"

Pete nodded and then added, "Have a nice time,"

"You too,"

"What, in this lovely town, how can I not?"

"This must be it," Said Pete, to himself by the door, because he had a habit of doing that.

And it must be it. After all, he followed the address, and there might not be a lot of houses around the local area that was had a garden of twisted topiary of hounds, not to mention an observatory tower with a globed glass window at the top.

He put the strange glowing package by his feet as he knocked on the door.

It opened just before his last knock, and a trembling face appeared.

"Yes?"

"I've got this package from Scientific Artefact Devices. It's for a Mr. K.Z. Limbic?"

The door burst opened, and Pete was welcomed to the site of a man with messy, frizzy grey hair and wearing a long coat with black and white patches sewn on it.

"Come in, come in," He said, a higher pitched quiver to his voice.

"I don't know, I will just give you this package and…"

"Ok, did I mention there are biscuits?"

"Well, ok then," Said Pete, following Mr. Limbic into the house.

"You don't mind if their dog biscuits, do you?"

Opal sat at her table with her tea. She looked out through the window and felt an odd sense of peace as she noticed the last darkening hues of the day and the last drizzle. It was a quiet moment. An inner, reflective moment where she was soon to fall into a lull of inner psychological protection and think about the pain. It gathered up inside her like a malevolent storm. She felt her eyes moisten and she wiped them and stifled a cry then pushed her cup of tea forward because at that point she just wanted to reject everything.

She looked around to see if anyone can see her and felt very self-conscious. All she saw was an old woman so engrossed in a book she hadn't noticed her, and the people serving were too busy cleaning.

She sniffled, wiped away her tears and smiled if only to bleed the pain out. It was if she was along and her pain didn't matter to anyone. And that was not the only time she had felt that. She felt better, in an odd way, that the pain that so eminently rose in her being was captured within her and could not be heard. Although sometimes it could break out, like a whimpering howl. That is why she tried to keep her smile the loudest thing about her.

"Help!" A man shrieked as he came into the shop, a grubby looking man in tatty clothes, "My mates been murdered, there was... there was... a Black Dog!"

"So, sorry again for the mess...."

"Oh, no it's fine it's... just fine, "Said Pete, eyes darting around the room, noticing the absolute mess of the small living room, things upturned, spills and all sorts of stuff left on the floor. He was sitting opposite the man in a small comely straw chair while the doctor was perched at the edge of a black stool like a demented parrot. He had the quirky diss-jointed movement of one as well, Pete noted.

"So how are you finding it here in our little village?"

"It's nice."

"Nice, yes," Said the scientist, sipping from his cup of tea. Pete's cup of tea was on the chair arm, next to the biscuit he politely took. He was hoping that his host would not have noticed that he daren't put the biscuit by his mouth, whether he was joking about it earlier or not.

"What do you know about the black dog?" Mr. Limbic ask, with narrowed eyes and a curl of his lips

"Well, I'm a cat person more myself,"

"No," Mr. Limbic said, then did a high-pitched eccentric, almost girlish laugh. "no."

"Ok, well, I will just be…"

"I meant depression, Peter, depression,"

"Oh well, I know someone who has dealt with it erm, pretty bad," He said, looking downward.

"And you, my dear Peter, do you suffer from this most indignant of maladies?"

"I don't even know what you what you mean."

"Good, good," Said Mr. Limbic, his eyes lighting up in a way that frightened Pete, "Step into my office, if you please, kind sir,"

Pete didn't object and followed. It wasn't because he wanted to follow this strange and possibly dangerous man; he just couldn't be bothered to argue. It had been a long day.

The study was a long room, walls covered in papers with sketches and writings that Peter would never try to decipher. In the center of the room was a massive blackboard with chalk on it.

"Depression has long been thought of by lesser minds as a disease, a chemical imbalance, but what if, good Peter, it was a force?"

"What?"

"A force, like a force of nature, like the force of evil itself, something more tangible, personal even, a force that like a parasite clutches onto its victims and drains them until the inevitable conclusion,"

"Well, I never thought if it like that,"

"I can tell," The professor said and began using the chalk on the blackboard, so the irritation of its monstrous sound overcame Pete's realisation of his slander, "And if it's a parasitic force, can it be removed?"

"Well, I…"

"Well I can say, that yes, it can, and has been," The professor continued using the chalk, the franticness of his strokes becoming unison with the franticness of his voice. "But there was, erm, an unexpected downfall,"

"Mmm mmm," Pete nodded, staring at his phone as he messaged Opal that he might be late.

"It killed people."

"Killed people?"

"Yes, I underestimated the strength of the depression connected to the subject, to which I created, what I like to think to call, due to my flair for linguistics, the Black Dog,"

"You've lost me here," Pete said, admitting that he didn't get it, but he hadn't been listening for a while, more thinking and worrying about Opal.

"Never mind, you don't have to listen, just to obey."

"What?"

"We will deal with this problem once and for all."

"We?"

"But now, unfortunately, the experiment B6 will gain another victim, the Black dog will kill again," Mr. Limbic said, stepping back from the blackboard. "Depression Incarnate!"

In white chalk shone the image of the bloodthirsty monster:

The Black Dog.

"Tell me please, what's really going on?" Opal asked the man as they walked quickly into town, turning street by street.

"It's a monster, a beast, a great big dog!" He cried out, further leading the air, "Or it could just be some fatal case of air pollution, who knows?"

Opal frowned a frown that was followed by a shriek as she saw the body. Slumped on the floor, was a greyish pallet to the skin and an expression of such misery that Opal had only seen a few times before; in the mirror on some of her darkest days.

"Did you know him?" Opal asked, checking his pulse.

"No, I just found him, miss, after the black dog attacked him," The man said glumly, "Then I poked him."

"You did what?" But Opal's question wasn't answered by the pokey stranger; it was answered by a howl.

"Oh no, the black dog it's coming for us, it's gonna kill us!" The stranger cried out, then ran past Opal through the streets.

Opal followed him, heart racing.

Through quiet street to street, they ran, through every twisting corner, the sound of the creature's ravenous cries catching swiftly on their heels.

Opal heard it's call, a rasping whisper in her head;

Give up

You will never win

Useless

Useless

Let me feast on your useless bones!

But Opal kept on running, the stranger doing so up ahead;

Until he reached a dead end. A red-bricked wall. An appropriate colour, Opal grimly thought. The stranger tried to desperately climb over it. Opal close her eyes tightly, hearing the voice shout in her head.

Useless

Useless

You have always been useless

But then Opal thought of something; she had heard of this beast before. This voice, this ever-pursuing creature. For such a long time. And she knew what to do.

Only good for the darkness

The eternal darkness

Where you will sink

And I will eat

Give in.

Opal slowly turned around. She saw a big black cloud tower over her, shifting into shapes she could not truly decipher, but may well have been claws and teeth.

Give in

Give in

You are nothing

You will lose

Let us kill you

Let yourself die

"No," Opal said simply.

The black cloud rose up above Opal and roared at her.

"No!" Opal cried out, a silent yet defiant tear rolling down her cheeks.

The smoke thing then shrunk to the size and form of a black dog, although it was still a large black dog.

It then growled and bared its teeth.

"Oh no," Said the stranger behind her.

The black dog galloped forward and pounced on the stranger, seemingly passing through him like smoke as he screamed. All was soon quiet, as the body, now more grey, and with the most miserable of expressions, slid down the wall slowly;

The Black Dog had feasted again.

"Are you sure I don't look silly with this hat on?"

"I think silliness is irrelevant in our current course of action,"

"Oh," Said Pete, the large glowing helmet with wires sticking out, that had once been in the package he had delivered to him.

They were in the big globed room on the houses highest point. It was filled with blinking electronics and whirring things. Pete was stood in the centre, wires connecting to the hat to all other the room.

"Since you told me so bravely didn't even know about depression, you sweet soul, you must be able to thwart it," He said.

"Okay," Pete said, not feeling he was able to argue.

"This thing, on your head, is a thought and feeling enhancer, this will help you battle the beast when we summon it"

"Yeah, well, what?"

"Do you have life insurance?"

"Yes, why?"

"Does it cover being mauled and possibly killed by an amorphized sentient being of literal homicidal depression?"

"Ermmm,"

"No matter,"

Pete began frantically texting on his phone when the scientist was not looking.

Opal touched the man's grey wrist. It felt cold and empty.

"I didn't get to know you," She said quietly, looking into his vacant eyes that stared ever forward, seeing nothing but darkness "And I never will, and I don't think I was ever able to... smile... at..." She stopped, whipping her eyes, slowly.

Everything was quiet. And calm. She was standing over a dead man, and she felt that everything should not be so calm.

But it was.

Then it suddenly became colder and pouncing out of the wall was the Black Dog. It jumped over Opal and she turns to watch it speed away into the distance.

She then turned on her mobile phone. That's when she noticed the texts.

"So, what do I have to do again?"

"Think big, happy, monster neutralising thoughts,"

"Oh, ok," Pete said and focused hard.

He didn't believe what was going on, but he was a bit drunk and game for a laugh, and, he didn't want to risk imminent death from that maniac.

There was, of course, a howl.

"What's that?" Pete cried out

"The beast approaches," Mr. Limbic said, then added, with childish glee, "Oh, I loved saying that!"

"What, you mean this Black Dog thing?"

"Yes. Now, remember, big, happy thoughts."

"Right," Pete said, concentrating so much he began squinting, "What's that?"

"Why do you have to repeat yourself, you're not a parrot are you?"

"No, look at that!" Pete pointed outside the globe's window. It was large black smoke, with glinting eyes and teeth and claws.

"Oh yes... I'd thought it would use the stairs."

"Doesn't look much like a... oh, now it does," Pete said, as the smoke formed into the shape of a dog.

It then leaped through the glass window, smashing through the glass as large gusts of winds also powered their way through, sending papers scattering, causing chaos.

"Ok remember, happy, happy thoughts,"

"It's getting really quite difficult to bloody do that now!" Pete called out, his voice distant beneath the oppression of the howls of the dog and the wind.

"Hmm, you don't seem to be having an effect on the creature,"

"Really, because usually, I'm quite good with murderous phantom dogs!"

"Right, not to worry then," Mr. Limbic then went to a desk and brought out what looked like a large metal syringe with a trigger.

"You're not sticking that thing anywhere near me!" Pete cried as the dog looked like it was going to leap into murder.

"It's not you, it's a quantified ant-depressant," Mr. Limbic said, and he pressed the trigger and a beam of silver light hit the dog, and it cried out as a force field formed around it. "That will only keep it still for a few minutes, in the meantime, we have to work out what to do,"

"Screw this, I'm going home," Pete said taking off his helmet.

"We will go home... After we've dealt with that Bitch,"

Pete and the scientist looked around and saw Opal at the door.

"How did you get in?" Mr. Limbic asked.

"I read Pete's text, I remember the address and the front door was open,"

"Oh. Sounds logical."

"Now, tell me what to do,"

"Opal, Oppy, we've got to go,"

"NO PETE, NO," Opal barked, then lowered her voice, "No one else must die, I must do this,"

Pete nodded, Opal caressed his face softly, then put on the helmet.

"Have you had experience of fighting a monster such as this?" Mr. Limbic asked.

"Oh yeah," Opal said, fastening the helmet on her head, "all my life."

"Good, because in half a minute it's going to be released,"

"I'm ready," Opal said, closing her eyes tight, as if for a prayer, "I'm ready," She said, opening them again and staring fiercely into the fathomless depths of the beast.

The neutralising power stopped, and the Black Dog was realised. It growled and then whispered

"I am the darkness, the emptiness, the filler of lost things, why things feel lost, we eat, we eat all the good, all that is happy, and the memories not fat with happiness we shroud in sadness, I am the Black dog,"

Opal looked back. And she smiled and said:

"I am Opal, and I know I will win, the way I have always won against you, no matter how you have hurt, how you have bitten. Because I don't wallow in the darkness. Sure, I wade in it occasionally, but I have risen through as many times as it has pulled me down. I don't let the depression beat me. There is good in the world. There is light. There is laughter. There is always someone in the world who will smile, no matter how crap their day. Day always follows night. There is, there is love," She said, looking at her boyfriend, and he looked at her. The bright light shot out and hit the Black dog as it howled.

Time passed.

Opal pulled off her helmet that grew heavy on her and fell into her boyfriend's arms. He then kissed her.

"Erm, I hate to break up this touching moment of love, but there we still have, erm… a bit of a problem…"

The shopkeeper smiled gently as the door opened to his shop.

"Hello," said a kind, soft voice.

"Hell…." The shopkeeper began until he saw the beast.

"No, it's alright," Opal said, holding the excited dog back with the lead.

"But it's not, the Black dog, my Black dog, it's returned, returned to kill me!"

"No, trust me, it's been tamed, your darkness cannot hurt you now,"

"Oh," Said the shopkeeper, breathing heavily, "How did you now the dog, the monster belonged to me?"

"Oh..." said Opal with a half-smile, "Just a hunch," she said with a half-life.

"And it can't hurt me anymore?"

"No," Opal fully smiled, "I will make sure of that."

"Good," Said the shopkeeper, and he beamed.

"What's your name by the way?"

"Philip,"

"Philip's a nice name,"

"So, did he try to kill you?"

"Shut up Pete," Opal said, then kissed him tenderly on the cheek as she got into the van outside the shop.

"I can't believe we've kept the dog, we're becoming a right Scooby Doo gang."

"You've always wanted a dog," Opal said.

"Yeah, but not like..." As if in response, the Black dog barked, making Pete jump in his skin, "Are we even safe with that?"

"Yes, of course, we are safe with her, and If not, I know how to handle it."

"If you say so." He started up the van, to which it then juddered to ignition, "So what are we going to call her? I think something along the lines of 'murderous dog monster'"

"How about Philippa, for short?"

"That's not…"

Opal smiled at Pete. He shook his head in weariness, then begrudgingly smirked back.

"Very well, Phillipa it is then,"

Phillipa barked as if an answer.

"Right then, let's hit the road. Me you, and you're previously amorphized embodiment of evil murderous depression, now known as Phillipa." The dog licked Pete's frowning face with slobbery glee, and Opal laughed and laughed.

END

This is Jonathan again with a poem about seeking solace in the smallest of memories. In this, a small carbonated drink is the anchor to the past.

Panda Pops.

Part of the pleasure

of my junior youth

was me in the corner

of a dusty hallway

cradling a panda pop

dissecting guileless prey

whilst numb lights

bounced off the ceiling

and walls;

me in the corner

sipping a synthetic bev

analysing the beauties

before me,

me, almost knowing I'd

be writing this poem

my self deprecatory

ways transformed itself

into adolescence

for instead of sitting

in the corner

I'd calmly rip apart

romantic ways

by use of memory

and knowing these

trite encounters

never seemed to last

almost like the bouncing

amber lights on the walls-

love-struck folk were dumb

and I was in the corner

swigging on a beer

laughing at the naivety

but unfortunately

my reproach was encroached

by Du Maurier's bestseller

pulling me out of my head

and into the centre of

the room.

Making me fall at last

for the sun, the rivers

the trees and the stars,

the centre of the iris

and the feeling of being

inside someone's heart

now I'm in the corner

again, wanting it back

wanting all the colour

to help me in my art

fighting the grey

awaiting a new day.

Another Poem from Barry it's tried and tested…

Beta Testing

Something is clawing

At the door

I have woken the monsters

With my waking

Vulnerable in my dreams

Female and unfamiliar

In a dark place

Catcalls

Come from somewhere

As I struggle on the ground

With garments

I do not understand

From this point of view

White noise on my screen

Wind rushing in my ears

This is

A hostile environment

I am being sent

From a place of safety

In a different boat

But no less confused

By the feel of engines

Throbbing in my bones

As the tide

Takes me to places unknown

I am not finished

This is a beta version

Blocking my progress

My waking has woken

The monsters

But I will not feed them

Any more

Catherine Whittaker with a great poem called 'Trapped'

Trapped

He faced the TV
hunched like a clenched fist
in a leather armchair,
a big man, thick framed glasses,
black hair sprouting on his fingers,
every muscle strained.
He stared at the screen
rooted in a fierce stillness.

I was scared of him.
I imagined him coiled like a snake,
venom inside and sudden attack.
I was a visitor, walked past him
nodding goodbye as I went.
In that week he stayed always the same,
unflinching, like a stone in a rapid,
T.V shouting its shifting stories.

I never heard him speak.

David Bradshaw again with a great poem about some-one, no doubt, we all know.

A Hollow Man

For a man of strong opinions,

He has nothing new to say,

As he just receives his wisdom,

From the papers of the day.

He's a man of contradictions,

So, he knows he's never wrong.

And he's always self-reliant,

For he thinks it makes him strong.

And he'd like to tell you something,

That he thinks you've never heard,

But his need for you to listen,

Makes his ideas sound absurd.

Oh, he thinks he's very clever,

And he thinks he's very smart.

But he'll play the fool forever,

He's a master of the art.

He's a man who likes to travel,

And he loves to see the sights.

Though his endless days are wasted,

And he rarely sleeps at night.

And he wanted to paint pictures,

And he wanted to make art,

And he wanted to play music,

But he never had the heart.

So, he lives his life of sadness,

Though he knows that it must end.

At best, his own worst enemy,

At worst, his own best friend.

Kevin Chorlton again…. little bit of trivia for you…. he used to be my boss…

Depression

I have got a little secret but I not know who to tell

The fact is that despite my appearance I don't feel very well

I have no obvious cut I have no broken bones

But despite the lack of evidence I still feel very down

I have taken all the tablets and I have had the counselling too

Yet my problem is till with me and I DON'T KNOW what to do

You see although my illness is very common people do not see it as problem

"get off your arse and stop being weak your no man you are just a creep"

Maybe the answer to my little secret is not to fret but just curl up in ball and wait for the sirens call.

Barry Fentiman Hall once more with a spirited poem…

I, ghost

I am the afternoon shadow
Cast long in corridors
Blood red with power
Where well fed heels
Sound on old stone floors

I am the bright skull smile
Offered in mute greeting
To twitchy assistants
On their third coffee
As the telephone rings

Annual leave behind them
And pictures of The Queen
Haunting strangers' lives
Marking births, marking deaths
And all the spaces in between

We are the ghosts of County Hall
Our letters in the trays
Change the course of lives
Unknown to the sender
In so many unintended ways

I, ghost, am merely messenger
With heavy bag I wheel
Weighted down with sorrows
But I am always fabulous
When they ask me how I feel

Here is Michelle Graham again. 'Hearing voices' is a common but all too distressing part of mental illness. If you suffer from this illness there is help there,

Here is a website that specialises and advises sufferers - www.hearing-voices.org

The ones

Hear the voices in my head, tell me evil things at night, I hear the voices in my head, can you save me from my plight.

They come they go, I try not to listen but they seem to know, they tell me to die, they say I'm not worthy.

I hear the voices, even though I'm breathing inside I feel as empty as a stone, as heavy as a stone.

Thoughts should come then they should go, but do they hell, they are my hell, a living hell inside the head.

The ones I have in my head, weigh heavy in my mind, taking control thinking out loud. The voices turn against my thoughts, battle lines drawn.

Voices with their tongues causing pain within, destroying, firing, confusing, causing the ones in my brain to explode

This is Miranda Wright again with a fantastic analogy about cars and age.

Clapped Out

He's got this old banger.

He's had her since 1981

And he suspects "one careful owner" was a lie.

She's full of rust, her bodywork is dented

And her interior is worn to shreds.

But then, she has done an awful lot of mileage.

For the last twenty years,

She's taken him everywhere,

And now, he looks at her, and wishes

That he could afford to trade her in

For something glamorous, fast and new

But anything like that is out of his league.

So, he will keep on running her into the ground,

And meanwhile, he will browse online

At shiny red sports cars

That he will never ever own.

Jonathan Terranova once again with a poem about the crutch that many use to overcome depression. A brutally honest piece about the panacea of drink.

Confession

I'm a functioning drinker.

I can't go home to my grave

without a litre of beer in my head

 I can't stare at that television set

or put that microwave meal in

I can't look into my fathers eyes anymore;

I only see my dead brother's bed

I drive my brain to each bar

expecting to find solace

and the sounds of night

I guess

help me cope

I turn up at work

crumbling at the temples

dreaming of eve

rescuing me

but situations cost you

so I'm staring into

the mirror where

my parents are still together

his lips

her cheeks

I can keep them together

strangulated over my skull

yet with all this shame,

pity and reluctance to change

I sense a bird up ahead

and it's looking out for me

This is Paul Richardson, in his own words;

After a period of deep depression, having always been an artistic, creative type of person, now involved in photography in a major way. I decided to look at poetry and how I could put that together with my photographs in some way.

I tried writing a poem then looking for a photo to enhance the poem, but it didn't work. Then I tried writing a poem about a photo I had taken and I got a beautiful result. The two for me came together so beautifully, it was like magic. So I started giving my photographs a new brightness with a poem.

Bringing the two together can make a photograph feel a really beautiful picture. So now I am spending my time not just looking through the photographs I already have but going out into the countryside looking for those all inspiring shots that will enable me to write more beautiful poems to great photographs of the landscape we enjoy.

This is a beautiful poem to Paul's love....oh, and wait for the end...

Hanna, My Love

O lovely morn, I lay awake

This beautiful, this lovely day,

I think it could be such a day,

One with goodness in its way.

As I lay in bed in thought,

Your eyes they turned and gazed at mine.

You crept up closer to my side

And stroked your body alongside mine.

I stroked your side, you arched your curves.

Your body rubbed against my side.

I stroked your side, you looked at me,

Your bright eyes slowly blinked,

You curled and rolled.

I smiled and caressed your curving back.

You rolled again and cuddled up.

And as I stroked across your brow,

I thought, that's Hanna, my love, my pussy cat.

Nick Fould's with a poem about that mode of travel where all life exists it's the wonderful zoo, the late bus.

Late Bus

Minding me own, late Friday night

Enter stagecoach, stagecoach stage fright

'You must be ravenous', She drunkenly squealed

Got summat for ya, all will be revealed

Stuffs a 9 inch pizza into her face

Come sit with me, I've saved you a place

Don't look son, don't catch her eye

Rough as a sheet, of coarse wet and dry

Quite appropriate it's fair to say

As she's rubbing me up, the bloody wrong way!

Staring out the winda, catches your reflection

Soon to be added to her collection?

Too late kid, in her web you've gone

Sez you're a dead ringer f' Simon Le Bon

Yeah that's it, try n look cool

Pull up the hood on your sweaty cagoule

She aint taking no for an answer

Says she used to be a go-go dancer

What she says, might not be the truth

Removing debris from behind a tooth

"Come on then, this is our stop"

Stumbles down the bus in a bit of a strop

Crikey me! So you know her then mate?

Oh dear, sorry, my big mistake

Bus pulls off, she's blowing ya kisses

I didn't realise that she's the Mrs!

Not minding me own late Friday night

Depart stagecoach, stagecoach stage right

Another fantastic poem by Tony Noon, a lament of a time going by.

LAMENT OF THE BOAT POET

We were an armada then.

Ship long sunk but still,

conscious of where we came from,

we pulled the same strokes

to drive us who knew where.

Destination less crucial

than shared pasts,

the rhymes and shanties

bound us, tided us over

amongst the dark waves.

Lately though my voice

reverberates on thinning air,

and fewer, ever fewer

join the chorus

Here is a short story by me…

It was first published in 2017 in my book. Tales of the Unaccepted. It was recently turned into a radio play.

It's about a witness…

Witness

She blustered into the kitchen, a china shop bull.

Even at this time in the morning, she was beautiful. She was a Tasmanian devil of shining hair and perfume spinning on a cartoon axis. What always hit me first was her smell, not just the perfume she wore, but her skin and hair, breath and perspiration. I drown in it ever time she's near, and I love her for that. Of course, I would not dare tell her and considering what was about to happen, in the next 20 minutes, I would never get the chance.

She didn't see me. Whether this was intentional or not, I did not know. I was, in this relationship, used to being ignored. This morning I didn't mind because I was busy enjoying my leisurely breakfast.

Laid out before I was sticky sweet cereals, bread and fresh butter, although there was always a choice, I must admit I do tend to gravitate to the sugary end of the morning's selections. Who doesn't love jam?

She seemed lost in her thoughts and leant over the kettle grumbling, 36 but she did look much younger. Slender and tall, she dwarfed me. She prepared coffee, one cup, I can never manage one myself, just the odd sip. She stared at her mobile, and I noticed that she was chewing her lip nervously.

The kettle's steamy siren broke her concentration; I couldn't help but noticed she jumped slightly and trembled as she reached for her cup. She poured in the hot liquid, stirred it violently and raised it to her lips, there; again, I could detect a slight quiver. She was nervous. I knew better than try to bother her when she was like this, so I carried on with my repast. A loud knock made us both jump; I thought I could see the door shaking with the stress of it.

She walked to the kitchen door and opened it slightly. The man forced the door open and using his shoulder barged his way into the house. Shocked, I was frozen where I was. The man was large; his teeth bared like a rabid dog, he screamed a stream of obscenities, machine gun menace in staccato spittle.

Surprising she didn't seem afraid in fact she echoed his anger, shouting furiously about his uninvited intrusion, he didn't appear to listen, ignoring her and walked over to her handbag on the kitchen table. She tried to stop him, but he pushed her roughly to one side. At this point I'd seen enough, I shouted for him to stop and get out. He was so wrapped up in his storm he carried on not seeming to hear me at all. He pulled out her phone and waved it in her face. Now he was ranting about some messages to his wife. Then it started to become a bit clearer. They'd been having an affair, he'd finished it, and she had decided to contact his wife.

What was that saying about a woman scorned?

He whirled and launched her phone against the wall; it smashed into the wall above me and shattered into a hundred pieces, communication cascaded and exploded all around me. I saw this all in exquisite slow motion. Luckily no shrapnel connected with me, but, like the coward I am, I stayed rooted to my position.

The staccato sound spurred her into action; she spun round and grabbed a large sharp knife from the block next to the kettle.

She brought it up in front of her and waved it in the man's face like a talisman warding off an evil spirit. A horrible rictus grin stretched across his face; it seemed to split his face in two. There was no humour in this smile, the meaty sneer of the confident carnivore.

He took the knife from her in one swift fluid movement that, to most, would have been impressive. I knew I could move that fast I just wished, at this moment, I had the courage.

She screamed at him; he maintained that terrible humourless grin. Her shouts came to an abrupt stop as he plunged the knife into her throat. I saw all this in terrible slow motion, the serrations like sharks' teeth gobbling into her flesh, the gout of metallic haemoglobin fountaining and striking the wall. It decorated the kitchen in her ebbing life.

She did more than fall; she seemed to crumple as if the blood kept her turgid, like a deflated balloon she sunk to the floor. I could tell she was dead before she embraced the cold tiles. The man showing no emotion or reaction to his deed turned and swiftly left the house. He exited as he had entered, slamming the door behind him.

Now it was my turn to be shocked into action. I flew to her side; of course, too late, life had left her. Blood pooled and congealed around her body creating a shadow in red. Its strong sweet smell mixed with her perfume. I let it wash over me a tidal wave of olfactory sea. God help me I found myself tasting it. I sobbed as I drank.

It was probably the shock, but I lost all concept of time, I slept, dreamless sleep. I was awoken abruptly as the kitchen door was kicked in. Thinking that the killer had returned, I retreated to my refuge of the kitchen table.

Three men walked in, two in uniform, one in a suit. The suited man barked orders "Get SOCO here Wilson"! The subordinate spoke into his crackling radio. In the gloom, they didn't see me.

The man in the suit fell to one knee, "stabbed to death, no sign of forced entry, she knew her killer".

He looked over to where I was and noticed the smashed phone. "Should be a SIM card in that, have it checked for messages" he motioned to the other uniformed man.

At this point I could be silent no more, "I saw it all!" I shouted.

No response, the Police Men didn't even acknowledge me. I'd had enough, I finally plucked up the courage I'd been lacking and decided to approach them. The man in the suit raised his hand and attempted to strike me, confused I fell back towards the window, "Oh and Wilson, open that window all we need is that thing laying eggs and maggots all over the place, it'll be contaminating the corpse."

The officer opened the window behind me, I felt the outside air seep in and ruffle my wings. They started to buzz as I sped up their movement, launching myself into the air I flew away.

End

Another poem by the wonderful Nick Foulds this one plays with the metaphor of 'patch.'

Patch

You can patch things up
But the holes still there
You can work things out
But you've got to care

You can steady the ship
Keep an even keel
You can work things out
But you've got to feel

Button your lip
Pull up your socks
Take a tip
Keep it in the box
Button your lip
Straighten your tie
My advice?
Ignore the lie

You can look surprised
Buyer beware
Keep your hearts receipt
Remember those lies

You can patch things up
But the holes still there
Couldn't work it out
Sad, that you don't care

This is Paul Richardson again with a haunting story cleverly constructed as a piece of poetry about his, strange walk.

My Strange Walk

I stood and gazed into the sky,

What a day, it seemed so bright.

Not a cloud, nor wind did stir.

It made it perfect for a walk today.

I set off down the country lane,

Then up the path to the wood ahead.

As I reached the woodland path,

Strange noises echoed in the air.

I looked around, no sight or sound,

But still the sounds kept on and on.

I moved on slowly in the wood,

To see what mysteries may unfold.

It was then I noticed near the ground,

A beautiful flower with a huge red bloom.

I knelt down low to see this flower,

I've never seen such a bloom before.

As I looked into its bloom,

It seemed to hold me to its side.

I seemed drawn to that bloom and flower,

As if to be swallowed by a UFO.

I suddenly realised, just an inch away,

I was a hard push to do it,

But I managed to be free.

How could this happen,

It's not really true.

Does this happen, it's really life,

I thought it was just in the films.

So careful on the pathway,

As I started to walk.

As I turned the next corner,

Not knowing what to find.

Do I look to the left?

Or do I look to the right.

Do I look straight ahead?

Where the pathway just goes.

At that point still wondering,

The noises that I hear.

I just dropped my great phone,

So had to reach down to the ground.

As I reached down for my phone,

A rush past my head.

Felt so close to me, rushed past me,

Like a jet plane above my ear.

I looked up but saw nothing,

No object in sight.

How could something move,

With that kind of speed.

I picked up my phone,

And started to think.

This place is so different,

So strange how things are.

I looked at the pathways,

Going back is the way.

But as I looked further,

The pathway to take.

I cannot see which way,

Will be the right way.

I turned so many corners,

Going this way then that.

This is terrible, it's awful,

I don't know what to do.

But just a minute my phone,

A walker's map, it did work before.

I picked up my phone, a signal I hope,

But there's nothing, it won't work at all.

I turned around a walking back,

My eyes checked with care.

After a while it seemed so strange,

There was nowhere I knew to go.

I then looked ahead to the rocks by the way,

They seemed to give more than a shine.

For as I drew near a door opened wide,

A notice that beckoned me in.

This is Tina Firthlock, in her own words -

I am a self-employed Artist delivering therapeutic and accessible art sessions for people with Dementia, Older Adults and Adults with Learning Disabilities. Prior to that, I spent seventeen years working with various charities in voluntary and paid roles within the UK and abroad, mainly supporting people who were experiencing Homelessness, Drug and Alcohol dependency or Domestic Violence, as well as working for Missing People and in all of my roles, I witnessed how mental health problems can develop and how devastating the consequences can be to both individuals and their families and how difficult and complicated it can sometimes be to offer the appropriate support. I have also had experience of mental health issues with close friends and family.

As for writing, I have been interested in writing since I was a teenager and have been on several short creative writing courses over the years, to endeavour to develop my work. I have recently formed an interest in writing poetry after attending a regular weekly creative writing group which has motivated me to finally achieve my writing dreams. I am currently working mainly on short stories based on my travels over the last 30 years and plan to publish my first collection 'The 27 Wanders of my World - Part 1' in Spring 2019, only a short 19 years after I started writing it and just before I reach the big 5-0.

This poem represents a 'light hearted' look at how we often have far too many tasks and responsibilities in modern society and how easy it is for things to spiral out of control when experiencing a mental health issue whilst trying to cope with even the basic things we all face in our daily lives.

The 'To Do List' Blues by Tina Firthlock

.

Feel free to sing in your head, the Blues riff at the end of each line in the verses, in the vein of such songs as Muddy Waters – Hoochie Coochie Man.

Make bed, order bank card (De de de de de)

Pressure Washer the back yard (De de de de de) etc

Take back mattress (it's too hard)

Try and find my ID card

Go online for food order

Pay electric, gas and water

Pay the rent (guess I ought to)

Make appointment for Doctor

But don't you know, I'm going to eat myself,

Eat myself a full box of French Fancies right now, instead of pills because, I think I know, I've got to endure the;

"I'm not ticking any stuff off my 'To Do' list" Blues

(Not even the important stuff)

Search for change under sofa

Research anorexia nervosa

Eat left over Samosa

Book tickets for Ponderosa

Ring Opticians and Dentist

Take some pills (feel horrendous)

(I've ran out) Go to Chemist

Book the kids in for Tennis

But don't you know, I'm thinking right now, it's only the chocolate, not exercise, that'll help me out, give me a thrill because I reckon, I'm positive, I am experiencing the;

"I'm not able to tick any stuff off my 'To Do' list" Blues

(Not even the vital stuff)

Got a headache, pains in chest

Stay laid down (I need bed rest)

(Tell the doctor) I feel stressed

Look up if I am de-pressed

Roman costume (Just make it)

Watch for Bailiffs (High Court Writ)

Buy a Cheerleader outfit

(Knock on door) Don't answer it

But you know, it's a drink, not therapy

That'll stop me feeling crappy right now

As I'm positively definite, I am suffering from the;

"I've no energy to tick stuff off my 'To Do' list" Blues

(Only the stuff that makes me feel good stuff.

Like buying Chocolate, French Fancies and booze stuff)

Brush your hair (it's a bird's nest)

(Find it hard) Just to get dressed

Replying to all those requests

Ring up now for the blood tests

Visit chemist for new pills

Go to gym on the treadmills

Contact CAB for help with bills

Too much of a good thing will make you ill (surely not)

But don't you know, I'm going to have to spend hours procrastinating, playing futile online games on my phone just because I know, without a shadow of a doubt I've been attacked by the;

"I've got zero motivation to, tick any stuff off my 'To Do' list" Blues

(Not even the truly urgent stuff)

This is a lady who wants to be known by her initials only

This is C.L.L. in her own words.

I'm a busy mum to two amazing children and lucky enough to be married to the most incredible man I've ever met. We live in a North Yorkshire village with our two cats and enjoy the country life. I enjoy a fulfilling career and run a business with my husband in our spare time. My hobby is writing, which I try to squeeze in at any opportunity. Life is always chaotic but I wouldn't have it any other way!

This is a wonderful idea write a letter to yourself...

This Time Is Different
By C.L.L

Only once I'd recovered did I see the extent of my illness. I wish I'd told someone about what was going on, been brave. This is the letter I would send myself back then had I known the future, instead I'll write it for you, in case you can relate and it brings you hope.

Dear Me,

I am you two years, nine months and twenty-three days later. We are okay. No, actually we are happy. As unbelievable as it may seem, we did it again. This time is different.

This time we don't cry. We don't fantasise about leaving in the middle of the night before anyone wakes up. We don't feel we've ruined our life. We don't hesitate picking up the knife when cooking dinner in case we hurt ourselves like we imagined. This time is different.

Having a tough birth and not being able to breastfeed isn't the universe telling you that you are a biological failure. We deserve to be a mum and our children adore us, we are their favourite human on Earth (but I don't admit that we know it to our husband). Cut yourself some slack, just because women have been doing it for thousands of years doesn't mean it's easy. You are allowed to feel traumatised, after all you nearly died- twice in fact. Maternal instincts do not have all the answers either, you'll learn this eventually. This time is different.

The four walls don't feel like they are choking us with claustrophobia anymore. We don't feel like a fizzy bottle of pop, shook with anxiety until we fear we may physically explode. Our own skin doesn't make us uncomfortable. This time is different.

We are connected. Connected to our babies; they fill us with awe, love and pride every day. We are connected to our friends, family and most of all our husband. Being with them brings us joy and excitement. We have a social life, even if it does include more play centre lattes than espresso martinis. This time is different.

I want to tell you that it gets better when you go back to work and regain your identity as an individual, with skills and knowledge that doesn't just involve benign things like 'top five ways to get crayon off a wall'. It isn't selfish to like work and it doesn't make you a bad mum, we are a more loving and inspirational parent because of it. This time I've retained that identity.

This time is different because I feel different. The grey veil that covered and stained every thought, action and memory hasn't descended this time. We see clearly, think clearly and feel clearly- it's a revelation!

I have granted us forgiveness. We haven't always been thoughtful to those around us or spoken kind words. We haven't always appreciated others or offered help when they needed it. You were too consumed in a fight to regain yourself. We are sorry for the impact we had though. Your friends and family still love you. Your marriage is still your solid cornerstone. Your children did not suffer any detriment. Let that give you comfort. The one who truly suffered at your hands was you, and we've forgiven ourselves for that too.

No one takes your children from you because you aren't perfect or sleep-deprived crazy. Our children are happy, creative and inquisitive. I don't want to mislead you, they are also cheeky monkeys and think nothing of having a full meltdown in the supermarket on a weekly basis, but we don't mind so much. I wish with all my heart that this was the experience we'd had the first time but it wasn't and I can't change what I couldn't control.

I am the mum I am because of what you went through. We are a happy and content woman. We are doing a great job. Hang in there.

Love always,
Me xx

Danielle Ramsay

Danielle Ramsay is a proud Scot living in a small town in the North-East of England. Always a storyteller, it was only after first wanting to be a filmmaker and obtaining a First Class (Hons) Degree in scriptwriting that she then went on to follow an academic career in literature. It was then that she found her place in life and began to write creatively full-time after being shortlisted for the CWA Debut dagger in 2009 and 2010, followed by being appointed as a New Writing Read Regional author in 2011. She is the author of five DI Jack Brady novels, including The Puppet Maker (2015) described by Martina Cole as "totally fabulous. I absolutely loved The Puppet Maker." This was followed by The Last Cut (2017); a dark, gritty thriller and the first in a new series featuring DS Harri (Harriet) Jacobs.

She has just completed her latest book, The Shadow Man which was described by Martina Cole as a: "fabulous read. Loved it!" An intense psychological thriller involving a forensic psychologist and a patient of hers known as 'The Doll Girl', who vanishes with dire consequences for those t

Always on the go, always passionate about what she is doing, Danielle fills her days with horse-riding, running and murder by proxy. An advocate against domestic violence for personal and political reasons, Danielle is the Patron of the charity SomeOne Cares which counsels survivors of domestic violence, rape and child abuse.

Here is a wonderful piece from the view of a sufferer.

Nothingness

I stand at the kitchen sink staring out the window.

I know the sun burns furiously; bleaching all in its wake.

Set perfectly against a tranquil sea of azure sky.

But I can't see it.

I can't feel it.

It is filtered. Restricted.

Mute. Grey.

Deafening in its lack.

I stand at the kitchen sink staring.

My hands pinned down as water drowns them.

But I can't feel them.

I can't see them.

Tears choke me.

They confuse me.

I feel nothing.

I stand at the kitchen sink.

I want to let go.

To plummet from this precipice.

But I force my hands down under the torrid rush of water.

Unable to stop crying.

I wait for it to pass.

I stand at the kitchen sink staring out the window.

I know the moon illuminates the evening sky dispersing the darkness.

That the stars are there. Somewhere.

I wait with my hands held down under the gush of water.

For the colour to come back.

D.R

This is Sam Fulton.

Sam is a talented young man. In this honest piece he writes about the struggles most young men face, where their place is within this world. Young men like Sam are at the greatest risk of suicide in our society. If this piece makes one other young man think, then Sam is a hero.

Life

Where is life taking me?
What do I want to do?

I spend my time waiting, hoping, wishing life would just give me what
I'm asking for, but how does life know?

What is life?
Is it conscious?
Does it understand what I'm thinking?

I spend more time debating these things than actually
chasing/attacking/devouring what I want from life. But where does
that leave me? In the same place, same spot, same time.
Do I really want what I ask, or do I just want an answer?

An answer to what?
Who is asking and why am I so desperate to know?

Life in and inconceivable mess and no one can tell you what you want
to know. You can think, live, breathe what you believe but life will
Never bring you it or peace.

Life is not what they give you in the media, not what you read in a
story or what you hear in music. Life is you.

Where do you go?
What do you do?

How do you get from A to B without tearing yourself through unadulterated pain and suffering and grief and stress and AHHHHHHH.

Life is what you choose. I struggle. You struggle.

I write this with a bottomless pit of sadness knowing I will never be where I want to be in life because I don't know where that is yet. It's a constant chase. A constant race. A constant never-ending cycle of 'who am I', 'Why am I here, 'what should I do?

The answer is simple. Look in a mirror.

Think of hating yourself, think of killing yourself, let it all pass. When all is said and done you're not looking through your eyes but through the eyes of everyone who has ever seen you.

You belong, you are needed and by the grace of God you are here to change something, anything, everything.

Be the change in one persona life and you will be the change you want. It's weird how you speak if others' lives but view your own as non-existent. If they have one, you must too.

Don't disobey, don't disregard, don't abandon. If you can see through someone else's eyes, they can see through yours.

Grasp what you don't have and live.

Make the grind and take the reward. Life goes on and so do you. I have faith in me, it took years, but I do. Have faith in you.

This is Jan Holliday in her own words.

I am 70 years old, I was made redundant (again) and went through self-neglect and all the rest. Started at a Writing Group, after much encouragement, I have not looked back (I wish). I am happier now and things are much better now.

Lady, Depression Hovers!

I can feel it like a noxious cloud.

Threatening to envelop and enslave,

I must take action, or drown.

Please, I beg, treat yourself with respect:

Do what has to be done,

Walk away from the rest.

Dust doesn't hurt, or eat anything.

Dishes in the sink, washing in a pile?

Dunk them in hot water,

Dormant, to soak until later.

Shower, bathe with scented lotions,

Dress up a bit, beads and lipstick

Perfume to give you a lift.

Go out, walking like royalty,

Head up, breathe in, blow out.

Look all around and about.

Shoulders back, pace evenly, at your pace.

From the door, down the path to the gate,

You're unique, be brave, think proud

Go somewhere, it's your world.

It belongs to you.

A Cafe, have a coffee, smile,

Smile at a stranger, say "Hello"

You may have met a friend,

That you don't know yet

Here is Sharon again with a lovely little chiller to make you shiver. Sit down, make yourself a drink and enjoy …… Platform 7

Platform 7

I caught this train every Friday, on the long journey back home. Two hours and seventeen minutes of sweaty bodies crushed together in the carriages, like the proverbial tinned sardines. The station announcer then decided to tell us that the train on platform 7 was running 45 minutes behind schedule. My shoulders drooped. The train on platform 7, or rather not yet on platform 7, was mine. This happened too many times; I already was penning my strongly worded email to Network Rail in my head.

I might as well get myself a coffee. Seeing as I've got the time. Again. I looked up and down the platform, which Costa had the smallest queue? And then I saw her. Alone. Further up the platform from everyone else. She was smartly dressed, a little old fashioned perhaps, but obviously good quality clothes, although surely that wasn't real fur at the collar? She had a small case and was stood at the edge of the platform. Too close to the edge in my opinion. She was very still, only her shoulders gently moving up and down. At first, I thought she had headphones in, then I realised that she was crying. No, sobbing was better. I smirked. It wasn't that bad the train being late! Then I felt bad. There was obviously something wrong. I had a quick look round but no-one else appeared to be looking at her. Should I go speak to her? Get her a coffee, maybe?

"The train on platform 7 is now running 50 minutes late."

"Christ above, I'll never get home" I glared at the nearest speaker, holding it personally responsible for the delay. I turned back towards the woman to see if she had heard. She wasn't there. I quickly scanned the crowd on the platform but couldn't see her. I stood on tiptoe, glad that I was 6-foot-tall, and looked over the heads of the other commuters, trying to see her. She wasn't there. Where was she? How could she have moved so quickly? I scanned the stairs and escalators. Nothing. I was confused and not a little concerned that she wasn't there. But what could I do?

Friday again. I stood on the platform, tensing myself ready for the announcement to say the train was late. I scoffed, a tiny noise escaping my lips. Wasn't it always the same? I peered up the platform, into the dark, to see if I could see the lights of my train; optimistic or foolish, I wasn't sure.

A movement caught my eye. It was the woman again, standing in the same place. She turned her head and looked up the platform, obviously wishing, like me, that the train would hurry up. She turned back, her head bowed, staring at her feet. I felt sorry for her, she looked alone and forlorn. Yes, that was the word, forlorn. I stared at her, hoping she'd catch my eye, smile maybe. But she didn't turn around.

"The next train to arrive at platform 7 is the 18.12 service to Liverpool."

Wow, it was on time this week! I could hear the lines singing as the train approached, and I could feel the crush of people moving towards the edge of the platform. I glanced at the woman. She didn't appear to be moving towards the carriages. She stood a little to one side. Oh well, I wasn't waiting to see which carriage she got on, I wasn't missing the chance to get a seat.

I was lucky this time; I managed to get a seat by the window. It was facing backwards, but at least I could sit down. I squinted out of the window, looking along the platform to see if she had made it onto the train. I didn't know why I was so drawn to her, but I couldn't help but check. She remained on the platform, still staring down at her feet. Why wasn't she getting on the train? I tried to get to my feet, I wanted to get to the door and call to her so that she didn't miss the train. Before I even managed to stand up the doors beeped to announce their closure and the train lurched forward. I checked again, she didn't even seem to notice that the train had gone without her.

It was Friday again. This week was different though. I'd spent all week thinking about the woman on the platform. I had to speak to her. I had to know why she didn't get on the train. I had to talk to her, even if that meant missing my train. Anyway, who knows where it could lead? She might go for a coffee with me whilst we waited for our trains.

Typical, I was late this week. As I came down the escalator to the platform, I could see that the train was already pulling up alongside the platform, my fellow commuters already pushing onto the overcrowded train. I could run and get on it, but I'd decided this week I was going to speak to her.

I walked past the throng and headed along the platform. Behind me I heard the train engine groan and shudder into life as the 18.12 departed in a haze of diesel fumes. I looked around and I could see we were the only ones on the platform. I realised then how this must look. She might be scared of me, a solitary man heading towards her. I stopped a few feet from her. I could see that her shoulders were moving up and down. Was she crying again?

I coughed gently, announcing my arrival. She didn't even look up. Was I doing the right thing? Maybe she did want to be alone. I glanced over my shoulder, the rear lights of my train disappearing into the distance. I'd got nothing to lose. If nothing else, maybe I could help her.

"Hi, are you ok? I've noticed you for the last few weeks and I just wanted to make sure you were ok. I thought you were going to get on my train, but I haven't seen you on it." I chuckled under my breath "I don't want you to think I'm a crazy stalker or anything, but are you ok?" My voice trailed off. She glanced towards me and I could see that her lips were moving, but I couldn't hear what she was saying. "I'm sorry, I didn't quite catch that? Do you fancy going for a coffee? Its a bit nippy stood on this platform. I won't bite I promise!"

I half-turned towards the nearest Costa. I glanced back over my shoulder. She'd moved one step closer to the platform, her case abandoned between us. I shivered, pulling my coat collar up. Something didn't feel right.

"I'm sorry, I haven't even introduced myself, have I?" I took a small step towards her, extending my right hand out. "I'm Russ. It's nice to meet you. Can I interest you in a drink? A hot chocolate maybe, to keep this bitter cold out." She looked at me again, her lips still moving. She looked like she was chanting. I could just see the shine of a tear as it rolled unchecked down her cheek. I gulped. This was not right at all.

"Look, I tell you what, why don't you wait here, and I'll bring you a drink. A nice cup of tea perhaps? I won't be long." I could see a policewoman just about to enter the cafe. Perhaps she could come and talk to her. "I won't be long, I promise."

I turned away from her. I felt in my pocket for some change, I might as well take her a drink as well as speaking to the policewoman.

"Can I have your attention? The train passing through platform 7 is the fast train to London. This service does not stop at this station." I could feel the platform moving under my feet as the train approached the platform. I turned back to look at her.

"No!" I could see her now, her toes over the edge of the platform, the train rapidly approaching. I tried to run back to her, but my legs felt like lead. I was running through treacle, despite the adrenaline coursing through my veins. "Look out, the train's coming!"

My words were lost as the train's diesel engine roared. She stepped off the platform just as it reached her. "No!" I screamed, my scream mingling with the train's warning whistle. I slumped to my knees, fighting the urge to vomit there and then on the platform. Why hadn't I waited with her? Why hadn't I touched her arm and made her come with me? Why, just why?

I pulled myself to my feet, fighting back the sobs beginning to engulf me. I had to see if somehow, by some miracle, she'd survived. I staggered to the edge of the platform. I peeped over the edge, my heart racing, frightened of what I would see.

She wasn't there.

I gasped. Where was she? Had the train dragged her body along the track? I scanned the tracks for her, something of hers, anything to show where her body was. Nothing. I turned to look for her case. It wasn't there either. I frowned and scratched my head. I was certain she didn't have it with her when she jumped. I didn't understand.

I realised that no-one else had come to her aid; in fact, I was the only person on that part of the platform. Surely someone else must have seen her? I had to find her, I needed to speak to someone here and they could contact the train driver. They had to check the line. The poor girl's family needed to know. They had to find her body.

I could still see someone in the cafe wearing a Transport Police uniform. I ran across the platform and pushed open the door, causing it bang against the door stop with a loud clang. The policewoman and the barista turned to stare at me.

"Are you ok, sir?"

"You have to help. I can't find her body. She's got to be dead. The train must have dragged her along. You have to help. You have to ring the train driver!"

Neither of them moved.

"Come on! Do something!" I yelled.

"It's ok sir, calm down. Describe to me what you saw."

I couldn't understand why the policewoman wasn't doing something. I paced in the small area in front of the counter, wringing my hands. The smell of coffee permeated the atmosphere, the hiss of the coffee machine barely audible over the sound of my shoes on the floor tiles.

"She jumped. I saw her. A young woman. Wearing old fashioned clothes. I've seen her every Friday for the last few weeks. And then this week she jumped. She's not there. I've looked. You have to find her! Why aren't you radioing through to someone? For god's sake come on!"

The police woman and the barista looked at each other and smiled.

"What's so damned funny? She's bloody dead and you're both laughing!" I could feel the spit on my lips, the heat in my cheeks and my heart beating so hard I was certain they could hear it.

Both their faces straightened, although I could still see the creases at the corners of their eyes.

"Come and sit-down sir. Charlotte, bring the gentleman a cup of tea. With a couple of sugars. Ok sir, sorry, what's your name?"

"Russ. Russ Banks."

"Ok, Mr Banks. Oh, here's your tea."

I saw the look that passed between them as Charlotte placed a steaming mug in front of me.

"Mr Banks, you're not the first that has spoken to me about this lady. She's here every week. Someone always sees her, standing at the edge of the platform, sobbing. I presume you saw her sobbing?"

I nodded, silently.

"Simply put, Mr Banks, she's not real."

My mouth dropped open. "Rubbish! I saw her, I was as close to her as I am to you. She was crying, and I could see her talking. Of course, she was bloody real!"

"Mr Banks, I can assure you, she is not. Look, let me explain." She leant forward, looking me straight in the eye. I shifted in my seat, this wasn't right, they needed to look for her.

"In 1956, Dorothy Russell jumped in front of a train. She had been jilted by her fiancé, Albert, at the altar. She never got over the shame of this. He had left her for her sister, Betty. Dorothy never recovered. Three weeks before

Albert and Betty's wedding, she jumped in front of a train. She was killed instantly, but her body was dragged along the railway line for over 100 yards. She is often seen at this time of year. Its the anniversary of the time she died. Some say that she is seen because what she did was illegal. You see, back then, it was a crime to commit suicide. But the poor girl couldn't live with the stigma of what had happened to her, so she jumped. Her sister and fiancé postponed the wedding and then moved away shortly after they got married. Liverpool, I believe. Certainly, they never came back here."

I slumped in my chair. "What were those names again?"

"Betty and Albert. Why?"

I felt sick. The skin on the back of my neck prickled. I could feel the heat rising to my face, my cheeks burning.

"Are you ok, Mr Banks? You look a little odd." I could hear her voice in the distance. I felt a little light headed. I gripped the edge of the table, my knuckles white with the effort, and answered her.

And here is a final one from me.

Once again, thank you to all that contributed to this book. Congratulations you are all now published writers.

This poem is dedicated to all of you, I know where you are, and I know where you've been. Hold on tight and be good to yourselves.

Neville

Curtains

I'm not good enough to breathe

Your air

Not true enough to take

Your stare

I'm a stain on humanities

Very bed linen

I never finish, start, always

Beginning

I don't want to live in my scar tissue

past

Always feel the damn

Outcast

I play the part and act the

Clown

But don't you rely on me

I'll let you down

I'm a sleeper a runner,

Denier, fake

I hide behind

This mask I make

Time is finite, it always

Was

The curtain will fall

I'll miss the applause

Published by Wonderdog Press via Amazon Books

First Published 2018

© Neville Raper 2018

E-mail – Neville.raper@gmail.com

Blogger – The Thoughts of Chairman Anyhow

Printed in Poland
by Amazon Fulfillment
Poland Sp. z o.o., Wrocław